M U R D E R
A T T H E
NIGHTWOOD BAR

A Pandora *Whodunnit*

Katherine V. Forrest is author of a number of novels, including *Curious Wine* (1983), *An Emergence of Green* (1986), and *Dreams and Swords* (1987). *Amateur City*, Katherine Forrest's first Kate Delafield mystery, was published in paperback in 1987 by Pandora in the Women Crime Writers series. Katherine V. Forrest lives and works in Los Angeles, USA.

London

MURDER AT THE NIGHTWOOD BAR

KATHERINE V. FORREST

London

First published in USA by Naiad Press in 1987

This edition first published in Great Britain in 1987 by Pandora Press
(Routledge & Kegan Paul Ltd)
11 New Fetter Lane, London EC4P 4EE

Set in Linotron Sabon 10 on 11½ point
by Input Typesetting Limited London SW19 8DR
Printed in Great Britain
by Cox and Wyman Ltd, Reading

British Library Cataloguing in Publication Data

Forrest, Katherine V.
Murder at the Nightwood Bar.—(Pandora
women crime writers).
I. Title
813'.54[F]   PS3556.0737

ISBN 0–86358–239–7

Pandora Women Crime Writers

Series editors: Rosalind Coward and Linda Semple.

In introducing the *Pandora Women Crime Writers* series we have two aims: to reprint the best of women crime writers who have disappeared from print and to introduce a new generation of women crime writers to all devotees of its genre. We also hope to seduce new readers to the pleasures of detective fiction.

Women have used the tradition of crime writing inventively since the end of the last century. Indeed, in many periods women have dominated crime writing, as in the so-called Golden Age of detective fiction, usually defined as between the first novel of Agatha Christie and the last of Dorothy L. Sayers. Often the most popular novels of the day, and those thought to be the best in their genre, were written by women. But as in so many areas of women's writing, many of these have been allowed to go out of print. Few people know the names of Josephine Bell, Pamela Branch, Hilda Lawrence, Marion Mainwaring or Anthony Gilbert (whose real name was Lucy Malleson). Their novels are just as good and entertaining as when they were first written.

Women's importance in the field of crime writing is just as vital today. P. D. James, Ruth Rendell and Patricia Highsmith have all ensured that crime writing is treated seriously. Not so well known, but equally flourishing, is a new branch of feminist crime writing. We plan to introduce many new writers from this area, from England and other countries.

The integration of reprints and the new feminist novels is

sometimes uneasy. Some writers do make snobbish, even racist remarks. However it is a popular misconception that all earlier novels are always snobbish and racist. Many of our chosen and favourite authors managed to avoid, sometimes deliberately, the prevailing views. Others are more rooted in the ideologies of their time and when their remarks jar, it does serve to remind us that any novel must be understood by reference to the historical context in which it was written.

Some of the best writers who will be appearing in this series are: Josephine Bell, Ina Bouman, Christianna Brand, Pamela Branch, Sarah Dreher, Katherine V. Forrest, Miles Franklin, Anthony Gilbert (Lucy Malleson), Hilda Lawrence, Marion Mainwaring, Sara Shulman, Nancy Spain . . .

Linda Semple
Rosaline Coward

The first novels to be published during 1987 are:

Green for Danger by Christianna Brand
Death of a Doll by Hilda Lawrence
Murder in Pastiche by Marion Mainwaring
and
Amateur City by Katherine V. Forrest

Our autumn 1987 titles are:

Bring the Monkey by Miles Franklin
Stoner McTavish by Sarah Dreher
The Port of London Murders by Josephine Bell
The Spinster's Secret by Anthony Gilbert (Lucy Malleson)
and
Murder at the Nightwood Bar by Katherine V. Forrest

See back of book for selected titles.

For Sheila:
Ah, sweet mystery. . . .

WITH LOVING THANKS

To 'Jason' — who has brought honor to her profession, who has given many years of her life 'To Protect and To Serve.' Her unstinting technical assistance was essential to the writing of this novel; her own high standard of excellence has added to it a deeper and truer dimension.

To Montserrat Fontes, Janet Gregory, Jeffrey N. McMahon, Karen Sandler, Naomi Sloan, Gerald Citrin — The Third Street Writers Group, whose talent and integrity continue to exact my best effort, whose generosity and caring nourish me.

To Detective Supervisor Mary F. Otterson, Madison, W1, for her ongoing support, and especially for that early and crucial validation of Kate Delafield which enabled me to see Kate's value and significance.

CHAPTER 1

Detective Kate Delafield turned off La Brea Avenue into a horseshoe-shaped enclave occupied by a motel and a variety of small businesses.

'So tell me about this bar, Ed.' She addressed her partner, Detective Ed Taylor, as she angled the Plymouth between the three black-and-whites blocking the road curving away from the street. 'This close to the station, it must be one of your hangouts.'

'You're kidding, right?' Taylor opened his door and peered up a steeply rising driveway leading to a shrubbery-enclosed parking lot. 'Private club, gotta be. Anybody'd be nuts to hide a bar up there.' Taylor pulled his bulk out of the car and straightened his yellow and green checked jacket. 'The Nightwood Bar,' he said. 'Sounds depressing as hell.'

Kate got out and hooked her leather-backed badge over the breast pocket of her jacket. Automatically she reached under the jacket to adjust her shoulder holster, thinking that she liked the name of the bar. The name felt weighted, significant.

She looked down the familiar Los Angeles street with newly perceptive eyes, assessing it as the focal point of the coming investigation.

Across La Brea, on the corner, a bright yellow fast food restaurant offered fried chicken and biscuits and gravy. The rest of that side of the block was fenced in with wire and dominated by a long garage of adobe and frame, so immaculately white it might have been a hospital ward for the damaged cars crowded around it. On La Brea itself, the

1

stream of cars slowed only momentarily at the sight of police vehicles splayed all over the off-street area.

Kate turned her attention to her own side of the block, stepping back to survey it, ignoring the knots of staring onlookers behind traffic barricades and yellow police tape. She spotted Deems and Foster half-hidden by a black-and-white, their blue-clad backs to her, questioning two swarthy young men of obvious Middle Eastern descent whose gestures eloquently conveyed bewilderment.

On one side of the steep driveway leading up the hill a dress shop was closed this early Sunday evening, as was the travel agency next to it. On the other side of the driveway, below the motel, a car rental agency and a mail box rental office were still open; the gaping window of an adjoining storefront displayed a For Rent sign. At each end of the block two other businesses catered to the automobile, one specializing in repairs to Volkswagens and Audis, the other selling brakes and shocks. A typical block on this section of La Brea in LAPD's Wilshire division – except for one element.

Kate examined the Casbah Motel, thinking that as many times as she had driven this street she had never really seen the motel for the anomaly it was amid all the varied small businesses and fast food restaurants on La Brea. It was built on the side of the hill, the exotic name contradicting the staid appearance: simple wide slat frame, dark brown, with a broad horizontal stripe of lighter paint running along under the second story windows. Tropical shrubs and palm trees with the thick, dusty, settled look of long existence decorated its street-facing side. A small cafe fronted the motel, the words Turkish Food on a sign the shape of a fez. Twenty-four units at most, Kate guessed, and none of that almost palpable sleaziness of the sex-for-an-hour motels. To her knowledge, the Casbah Motel was not among the Division's hot spots.

Apparently the parking lot on the hill served the motel, the cafe, and the Nightwood Bar. Kate ducked under the yellow tape and walked up the steep hill, pressing her slick-soled shoes firmly into the rough asphalt for better traction, grinning at Taylor's wheezes of exertion.

A coffee-brown frame building with a roof of black-brown shingles was separated from the parking lot by an expanse of brilliant white ornamental rock. Clusters of low fir trees grew out of the crushed rock, vivid green against their background. The lone front window was lit with neon letters in lavender script: *The Nightwood Bar*.

'Weird,' Taylor commented, 'but nice and neat.'

The parking lot, containing perhaps a dozen or so vehicles on its motel side, extended back and behind the Nightwood Bar, a section of the lot not visible from where Kate stood. Several dozen spectators, presumably patrons of the hillside businesses, were clustered across from this section on the motel side, behind another barricade of yellow police tape. Kate rounded the far corner of the dark wood building, and stopped.

Like any other crime scene, the area had been cordoned off. Less typically, there was no designated pathway to the corpse, a figure in white at which Kate cast only a gauging glance. An asphalt parking lot did not present the same problems of scene preservation as a vacant lot or a public street but, Kate thought disapprovingly, precautions were no less vital. Stepping to the edge of the waist-high yellow tape stretching from the corner of the Nightwood Bar to the Casbah Motel, she evaluated the area.

The crime scene was a rectangle accessible from only two sides – the parking lot and the back door of the Nightwood Bar. The parking lot was separated from the heavily wooded hillside by a high redwood fence along its side and outer perimeter. Within the rectangle were three objects: a trash dumpster, a beige Volkswagen van of sixties vintage with its side door slid back, and the white-clad corpse.

'Sergeant Hansen,' Kate called to the knot of police officers gathered around the back door of the Nightwood Bar. The stolid Hansen nodded to Kate and Taylor and made his way over. 'I want a path.' She gestured. 'Diagonal, from that end.'

He nodded again. 'We waited to see what you and Ed wanted, Kate. The bar owner found the victim, Deems and Foster took the call, I looked at her. Then we sealed it all off.'

'Good work, Fred. Excellent.' As team supervisor she was pleased to have an apparently intact crime scene, and pleased she had not begun this investigation with criticism, even if

Hansen's history of misconceived police procedure warranted such criticism.

Hansen looked at his clipboard. 'We don't have much yet. The victim is Dory Quillin.' He spelled both names. 'Twenty-one, the bar owner says. Doesn't look it, though. She looks –'

Hansen's voice seemed higher pitched than usual and Kate glanced up from her notebook. His eyes were focused on a spot somewhere over her shoulder. He said, 'I don't know, Christ, she looks like – she's just a kid.'

The usually dour Hansen had been involved with innumerable investigations of deaths of young victims. Obviously, something about this homicide had touched him under the toughened defenses of his fourteen years in police work. She knew he did not welcome this vulnerability any more than she would. She said briskly, 'So what else have we got?'

Hansen again looked down at his clipboard. 'Crushed left temple.' His voice strengthened. 'Baseball bat, it's at the scene. Aluminum.'

'Recent?' Taylor had not looked up from his notebook.

'An hour at the very outside, from the look of her. And she'd just returned from playing baseball. She –' Hansen broke off.

Taylor said impatiently, 'So? We got suspects? Witnesses?'

Again Hansen's eyes focused on the spot beyond Kate's shoulder. 'Lots of possible witnesses. All of them women, all of them patrons of this bar, Ed.' He waited until Taylor looked up at him. Then he gestured toward the Nightwood Bar. 'It's a . . . women's place.'

Involuntarily, Kate turned to stare at the Nightwood Bar. *A lesbian bar.* She hadn't been in such a place in years, years and years, since. . . .

She wrenched herself back, concentrating on Hansen's words. 'We've interviewed everyone, taken names and drivers' license numbers, done field interviews – the FI's aren't much help. Except for the bar owner, everybody's uncooperative.'

Taylor scratched his head, then pulled strands of lank blond hair across his bald spot. 'What about Deems? Would they talk to Deems?'

'With her they got hostile.'

Taylor groaned and rolled his eyes. 'I don't care if they're lesbians. I don't give a fart if they're Martians. Why does everybody have to be so goddam nuts?'

'Any persecuted minority,' Hansen intoned as if quoting from a text, 'tends to act with hostility toward the symbols of its persecution.'

'Shit,' Taylor snorted.

Kate grinned at him. However gracelessly, the issue of what these women were had been brought quickly into the open, and she was grateful. She said to Hansen, 'But the bar owner did talk to you?'

Hansen glanced at his clipboard. 'Magda Schaeffer.' He spelled the names. 'I got that from her business permits, not from her. She got a little more cooperative when I suggested there might be grounds for busting her.' Hansen's face again took on grimness. 'For serving minors. The victim, Kate, if she's twenty-one I'm —'

'False ID,' Taylor said in a bored tone. 'Bet we find it on her. Got anything else? Where she lives?'

'Right there.' Hansen pointed to the van. 'The Schaeffer woman says she parked it here mostly, or at the beach.'

Kate studied the battered vehicle. 'We'll impound it. Parents? Relatives?'

'Parents — West Hollywood, the Schaeffer woman thinks. The other women here claim to know the victim only casually. And that's all we've got so far.'

Kate looked at the Casbah Motel, its L-shape framing the opposite side of the parking lot, and at the blank squares of beige curtained windows. She gestured. 'Who've you got over there, Fred?'

'Davis and Ploski.'

'Deploy every officer you can spare, I'm sure they'll allow us a permissive search. Have them interview everybody they can find. A motel, Sunday night — people will be checking out. Get addresses. Make sure you have the license plates of every single vehicle in this lot and in the off-street area down on La Brea. The motel registration, we can work with that, too.' She said to Taylor, 'Let's get started here, before we have the lab people all over the scene.'

In her notebook she made a quick sketch of the rectangle, the position of the dumpster, the van, the body. She recorded

5

the time she and Taylor had arrived, 7:13 pm, and the date, June 16, 1985, and the approximate temperature, 70 degrees.

Skirting the edge of the yellow tape, moving past spectators who shrank back as if to avoid infection, Kate and Taylor walked to the far end of the rectangle. Kate entered first, Taylor waiting for her signal. She moved carefully, in a straight line toward the van, scrutinizing the ground with each step.

The parking lot was unusually clean. A few scraps of fast food wrappers had drifted against the fence, but most of the debris has blown in off the hillside — leaves, pine needles, twigs, deposited in patterns by eddies of wind. She bent several times to examine cigarette butts and match sticks ground into the pavement, days old from their state of decay. The killer or killers had left a signature — all killers did — but it was unlikely, Kate reflected, that that signature would be found here in the open.

As she glanced around at what appeared to be the usual oil stains on the pavement, her glance froze on staring silver-blue eyes.

Dory Quillin's face was the color of pale wax, framed by white-blonde hair so fine it stirred in the faint evening breeze. The delicately wrought face, the small, tender mouth, reminded Kate of the exquisite perfection of an infant's features. But it was the wide silver-blue eyes that held Kate; they stared at her in supplication, in bewilderment.

Kate tore her own eyes away. Composing herself, reminding herself that the descent into death could freeze features into any configuration, she completed her scrutiny of the oil stains. Concentrating on placement of her steps, so crucial to the preservation and collection of evidence, she halted before the body.

The white clothing was a baseball uniform, a black stripe down the side of the pants, no lettering on the front of the jersey. Both arms were outstretched and both legs drawn up, the cleats caught in the pavement, as if Dory Quillin's last act had been an attempt to rise, to reach for her killer. And with those outstretched arms and that unbelieving face, she had died. . . .

A kid, Hansen had said in his inarticulate, unwilling grief.

Her white clothing added the greater symbolism of innocence to her youth and beauty. And those eloquent eyes told Kate that she could not comprehend her betrayal.

At a cautious distance Kate lowered herself to one knee. Dory Quillin's head was in three-quarter profile, the trauma to the left side partly concealed but graphically conveyed by the liquid pool that lay darkly under the declivity along the angle of forehead. Kate did not have to see the entire wound to know how it would look, the swollen edges, the surrounding tissues filled and black with blood.

Wishing with all her soul that she could reach over and close those unbelieving silver-blue eyes, Kate forced herself to examine her. No visible marks on any of the exposed skin, and the baseball uniform seemed to be intact; apparently there had been no added violation of Dory Quillin. She wore a digital wrist watch with a plastic strap – worth no more than a few dollars, Kate judged – and a pinky ring. The palms of both hands were upturned, and Kate could not determine if the ring had a stone of value. The short rope chain around the neck was gold. The jaw and neck, places where rigor mortis usually began, appeared still soft and pliant. Skin surfaces were insufficiently visible for telltale bluish or reddish signs, but lividity seemed unlikely.

Hansen was right; this homicide had occurred very recently. The killer of this woman-child could not be very far away. Perhaps even right here, in that crowd of avidly staring faces across the parking lot. As she signaled for Taylor to join her, she studied and committed their faces to memory. She would have Shapiro, who would arrive momentarily, work in some shots of them as he photographed the general area.

She watched Taylor following her path, placing his big awkward feet down carefully, double-checking, as he was supposed to, the terrain she had already studied. Then she watched him look down at Dory Quillin, watched him push his fleshy lips in and out. Ordinarily she only mildly disliked Taylor's gallows humor at a death scene; it distracted, lessened some of the grimness and tension. But if he offered any ghastly joke now, she vowed she would hate him forever.

He looked up at her silently; and his soft brown eyes mirrored mourning.

She said quietly, 'All of us are supposed to be God's children. She looks like one.'

'We're all God's assholes.' His voice was a resonant growl. 'Or we wouldn't do the shit we do.'

She turned toward the van. An aluminum bat lay in its shadow. She looked at the bare metal of the handle. Such a surface could hold a print. More than one person might have been involved in this homicide, but only one person had struck the blow. But many hands had held this bat before it had become a murder weapon . . . Still, there was hope.

For several minutes both detectives wrote in their notebooks, Kate recording in detail the position and appearance of the body, the condition of the clothing, the size and shape and degree of blood coagulation, her overall impressions.

Moving carefully, she stopped a judicious distance from the bat; Taylor hunkered down beside her. The shiny bat was darkly stained on one end; bits of dirt clung to the fouled area.

Taylor pointed. 'Looks like it was dropped, maybe right there – that could be a mark on the pavement, a bloodstain. Then it rolled over here.'

Kate studied the bat, the van, the position of the body. 'Maybe. Could have been thrown, too. Bounced off the van and back here.'

'There'd be a dent in the van – not that you could tell. But it would make a hell of a racket, somebody would hear.'

'Maybe somebody did.' But her instincts told her the killer had simply dropped the bat and fled. Again she studied the scene. 'From a blow like that, she'd fall like a stone. From the bloodstains she didn't move much.' Kate gestured. 'I'd say the killer stood about there.'

Taylor rose. 'With the wound on the left side, we got ourselves a right-handed batter.'

Had he not taken a few swings with an imaginary bat in demonstration, had he not grinned, she might have forgiven him. Five minutes, Taylor could allow Dory Quillin no more than five minutes of dignity. Too occupied wi. a despising him to reply, she made her way over to the van.

8

Both detectives peered into the open door. The back window was curtained in dark blue fabric with crisp white polka dots; matching curtains partitioned off the cab of the van. The back seat had been removed, the floor of the van was crowded with the possessions of Dory Quillin: a rolled-up sleeping bag; a wicker trunk, presumably for clothes – several T-shirts, neatly folded, lay on top of it. In a far corner, on flimsy shelving, dry foods were lined up – bread, crackers, granola bars, canned goods, a few plastic plates and cups. Squinting, Kate made out a bag of cat food under the bottom shelf next to a tiny hibachi and barbecue briquettes. Several dozen paperbacks were stacked against a small metal table which had apparently been used as a desk; a yellow legal pad lay face down upon it. Just inside the door a baseball glove leaned against the wall.

'Doesn't seem disturbed,' Taylor said.

Kate nodded her agreement. She was thinking of her own apartment in Santa Monica – a living room, bedroom, convertible den, not to mention a bathroom. Probably eight hundred square feet, altogether. Dory Quillin had lived in less than thirty square feet.

'The gang's all here,' Taylor announced, inclining his head toward the Nightwood Bar and the group gathered along the yellow tape. Both detectives made their way back along the trail they had blazed, toward the team that would begin processing the area.

Shapiro gestured toward the hillside and said unsmilingly to Kate, 'I suppose you want photos of every leaf on every tree.'

Kate answered the thin, bearded photographer evenly. 'I wouldn't mind you working some shots of the spectators into your backgrounds.'

'Sure.' Shapiro shrugged and grinned, and placed his case down on the pavement.

'Do us another favor,' Taylor said, 'try not to step on the victim till the coroner gets here.'

Kate nodded to Hansen. 'All yours, Fred.' She knew he would section off the crime scene and have his officers meth-odically conduct a thorough search as Shapiro photographed the scene. 'We'll be back when Everson –' To her consternation, her voice cracked.

She had remembered the autopsy. She turned her back on the body of Dory Quillin as if that act could prevent those silver-blue eyes from filling her mind. Not only would she carry with her the indelible vision of that face, she would have the horrific memory of that tender body on an autopsy surgeon's table. . . . 'We'll be back when Everson examines her,' Kate said firmly.

She snapped closed her notebook and stuffed it into her jacket pocket. Not for her to break the cardinal rule of police work: objectivity. Not for her to become obsessed with Dory Quillin. . . .

She looked up to find Hansen staring at her. Kate met his dark eyes and smiled faintly.

'Come on, Kate,' Taylor said. He grinned and jerked a thumb at the Nightwood Bar. 'Let's go in and charm the hell out of all those unfriendly women.'

CHAPTER 2

'What the hell kind of bar *is* this,' muttered Taylor.

Casting the most cursory of glances at a large room unusually bright for a bar, Kate did not reply. The greater imperative was to gather her wits, to assess the ten women clustered along the curved dark wood bar. Taylor's presence only added to her tension.

Where does my integrity begin and end? What if someone asks pointblank if I'm a lesbian?

They won't ask. She was looking into the faces of the women at the bar. *They don't need to.*

She felt stripped of her gray gabardine pants and jacket, her conservative cloak of invisibility in the conventional world. In here she was fully exposed against her natural background.

She recognized aspects of herself in each of the women staring back at her. In the assertiveness of one woman's posture, in the stocky build of another, in the untouched gray of a short hairstyle in the practical clothing and unmade-up faces and serviceably pared nails. . . .

With ingrained habit she noted that two women were black, two Hispanic. Three wore baseball pants and shirts similar to Dory Quillin's except these were in colors. Others wore pants and shorts, with shirts and T-shirts. A fat woman in a paisley skirt and peasant blouse sat with legs crossed, the skirt hiked above dimpled knees.

Their direct, perceptive glances penetrated her like an X-ray. A plump woman in white shorts and a blousy pink T-shirt, hoops of gold dangling from her earlobes, leaned over to whisper to her companion, a black woman with hair so

11

short it could not have been more than half an inch long. The black woman grinned and nodded.

'Which of you,' Kate said in the most commanding tone she could muster, 'is Magda Schaeffer?' She was braced and ready, expecting the murmuring wave of amusement at the low tones of her voice.

The burly woman who got up from a bar stool was perhaps fifty-five, with a whitening thatch of hair that looked self-cropped. Her lavender T-shirt was tucked into knee-length shorts with more pockets than Kate believed possible on an article of clothing: zippers covered the entire front and sides, with loops of fabric at each side, presumably to hold a flashlight or hammer. The woman crossed heavily tanned arms and studied Kate with deepset, hooded dark eyes.

'You're Magda Schaeffer?'

The woman nodded expressionlessly.

'I'm Detective Delafield. This is my partner, Detective Taylor.'

Again the woman nodded.

Would anyone in this room ever speak? Would they never stop their staring?

'I've already answered every conceivable question,' Magda Schaeffer said. The voice was soft; Kate had expected masculine gruffness.

'We need to go over details again, perhaps a number of times.' Kate raised her voice to take in the room, launching into her explanation of procedure with a sense of relief at this familiar ground. 'One of you might have a piece of information more important than anyone can see right now –'

'Bullshit.'

The speaker lounged on a stool at the end of the bar. A navy blue yacht cap was pulled down over her sharp, hawk-like features, cutoff jeans exposed thin but muscled thighs, the sleeves of a blue-checked shirt were rolled to the elbows.

She jabbed a finger at Kate but directed her words at Taylor: 'You think bringing a sister in here makes some kind of difference to us?' she barked. 'She's sold out to her own oppressors.'

Taylor cast an astonished glance at Kate.

The woman glared at Kate. 'Enjoy being one of the boys? Kicking your own sisters around?'

Kate said evenly, 'I don't kick anyone around.' She knew she must use diversionary tactics, break up this group, separate them before they solidified in their hostility.

'Patton,' Magda Schaeffer said, walking toward the woman, her hands on her hips, 'you cool it. You lay off all your political shit for just these few hours out of your life so these people can do their jobs and get out of here. The sooner they finish the sooner they'll be gone.'

'Dory's a dyke,' Patton said bitterly. 'Whoever killed her — he'll end up getting a nothing sentence in a cushy cell just like Dan White.'

Magda Schaeffer shook a finger at her. 'Patton, I'm warning you —'

'Cops never catch anybody anyway,' said the fat woman in the paisley skirt. 'Took three million of 'em to find the Hillside Strangler. Every cop in the whole country couldn't find Patty Hearst.'

Taylor strolled over to Patton. 'We'll be more than happy to listen to anything you have to say,' he said, standing close to her. Kate was well acquainted with the tactic; Taylor often used his beefy bulk to dwarf, intimidate a witness, all the while speaking in what he called his jest-folks voice. He continued, 'If you'd kindly wait till we talk to you, Miss Patton —'

The room erupted in guffaws. Patton pushed her yacht cap back and leaned against the railing of the bar looking up at Taylor, shaking her head, her smiling gaze drifting over him as if any conversation was clearly a waste of time.

'Do you live in some kind of time warp?' Magda Schaeffer snapped at Taylor. 'Does Patton look like she wants to be called Miss Patton?'

'Procedure,' Kate said succinctly. 'No offense intended to anyone. What would *you* like to be called?'

'Maggie,' the bartender answered with an almost imperceptible smile that was like a friendly clue. Kate felt suddenly warmed by her.

'We'd like to look over the bar,' Kate said. 'To orient ourselves.' At this moment it seemed more judicious to remove herself and Taylor than to break up this group. Afterward they would interview the women separately.

'Anything you want,' Maggie said with a vague gesture toward the wall behind the bar. 'Business permits are over there.'

The bar counter was an elongated curve, stools along its entire length. At the end sat a coin-filled glass bowl with a neatly inked sign: AIDS PROJECT L.A. Behind the bar, next to a blank television screen high against the wall, a long banner read: ALIVE WITH PRIDE IN '85. A large kidney-shaped mirror was surrounded by lavender lights, *The Nightwood Bar* written across it in script letters similar to the lettering Kate had seen in the window, but in painted ceramic.

'You run a strange place, Maggie,' Taylor said.

Kate was irked, both by his comment and his tone, which seemed to her offensively familiar and condescending.

'I guarantee you,' Taylor said, 'this is the only bar in the world with a bookcase.'

Kate walked across the room, looking around her in increasing amazement.

The bookcase was large – four crowded shelves perhaps ten feet long, toward the rear of the bar beside a pool table overhung by a tiffany-style lampshade. Behind the pool table were three tables, each with a different game set up: checkers, chess, a Scrabble board. Another table contained stacks of magazines and crossword puzzle books; and beside it, another held several decks of cards and a pink box; Kate made out its lettering: *Gay Trivia*.

Across a dance floor not more than twelve feet square, two other tables were set up for backgammon. Against the far wall of the dance floor a high narrow counter was fronted by two stools, a video game at each. The jukebox, alongside a cigarette machine, was dark. The entire room was decorated with leafy plants flourishing under generous track lights.

Incredible, Kate thought. If only there'd been a place like this when I was coming out. . . .

'It's the kind of place I've always wanted,' Maggie said. 'It's not a pickup joint – plenty of places in town for that.' She was addressing Kate, the angle of her body shutting out Taylor. 'Any woman who comes in here, she's not locked

into just drinking or dancing or playing pool. She can sit by
herself and read a magazine or a book or play cards with
somebody or whatever.'

Maggie's tone was low-pitched and earnest. 'Hell, I'm just
as happy to serve coffee or soft drinks as booze. We're busy
Friday and Saturday nights, but my crowd is mostly an older
crowd and mostly regulars. They come in for one thing —'
She spread her hands and finished with quiet emphasis, 'To
relax and be themselves.'

'Was Dory Quillin a regular?' Taylor asked.

Kate was pleased that Taylor had refocused this interview;
it was too perilously easy in these circumstances to have
her own concentration fragmented. Gesturing to Taylor and
Maggie, Kate pulled out a chair from a nearby table. The
three of them sat down.

'A semi-regular,' Maggie answered Taylor's question,
propping a Puma shoe on the unused chair. She lit an unfiltered Pall Mall. 'She hit most of the bars, like a lot of the
youngsters do.'

Taylor was trying to fit his bulk into the small wooden
chair. 'How long did she park on your lot?'

'Nine, ten months. You detectives must want some coffee.
Roz,' she called without waiting for an answer, 'bring us
three coffees, would you?'

'Thanks,' Kate said. 'Then you must have known her quite
well.'

'Actually, no.'

'She parked on your lot.' Taylor's skepticism was evident.
'She use the john in here too?' As Maggie nodded, Taylor
stated, 'Anybody'd think you were pretty tight with her.'

Again Kate was irked, reading the insinuation of sexuality
into his words. Maggie shrugged and drew smoke deeply into
her lungs. 'No, I just felt sorry for her. Did you look at her
out there?'

'Yes,' Kate answered for Taylor, 'we did.'

The coffee arrived, Roz serving the three mugs from a tray,
moving briskly away when the detectives declined the offer
of cream or sugar.

Maggie crushed out her cigarette and looked up at Kate.

'If you saw Dory then you know. A lost child. Out on her own, just her and that van –'

'Think she was really twenty-one?' Taylor asked casually.

'She had proof.'

Taylor nodded.

Maggie sighed. 'Hell, I don't know. I don't think so. God, she looked about twelve. But a lot of them do. The older I get, the younger everybody looks. Letting her park here was a little thing to do for her. And it was reciprocal anyway. Even though we close at two, I need some kind of protection after hours, the place is too far out of the way. My last watch dog gnawed through his leash and took off, Dory offered to stay for a while. She's been here ever since, not every night but enough. . . .'

Maggie's wide mouth twisted down at the corners. She ran a hand through her coarse white hair. 'I thought she'd be safer here than . . .' She made a dismissing motion, a gesture of futility.

'You put a hell of a lot of trust in someone you hardly knew.' Taylor did not look up from his notes. 'Giving her a key to this place – all this booze.'

Maggie gripped her coffee mug in strong, rough-skinned hands. 'You make judgments, you trust people. How else can you live? I'd have known if she ever did anything, took anything. She never did drink much . . .'

'When was the last time you saw her alive?'

'When we left the ballpark.' Maggie's voice was terse.

'Which one?'

'Plummer Park.' Maggie turned to Kate. 'The rest of us agreed to meet here, have a few beers. Dory said no, she had things to take care of. I heard her pull in back, but she didn't come in. Around six o'clock I walked out there to toss some trash –' The firm voice faltered.

Catching Taylor's eye, Kate signaled with an inclination of her head to give Maggie some moments to compose herself. She caught up on her own notes, intrigued by the idea that perhaps Maggie's manner might be a deliberate camouflage of depth and intelligence.

Kate asked, 'What time did you hear the van pull in, do you remember?'

'About five-thirty, maybe a little after.'

'When did the rest of the group arrive?'

'Within a few minutes of each other, we were in different cars.

'Right, of course,' Kate said with a nod. Maggie smiled at her then, the harsh features softening into a wreathing of fine lines around her mouth and eyes. Resisting an affinity for her, Kate continued soberly, 'The women here now, were they all here when you discovered the body?'

Maggie nodded, and Kate asked, 'The bar opens at five?'

'At four, Sundays.'

'Then someone was here before you arrived, tending bar.'

'Roz. She's my relief bartender. Only five of us were at the ballpark, you see. Ash was here and so was –'

'We'll get those names from you in a moment,' Kate interrupted, making rapid notes. 'We need to know about the circumstances after you arrived. Did anyone leave?'

'No. And that's definite. Even when the place is packed I keep close tabs on what goes on in my bar.'

Taylor said, 'Are you telling us none of these women could've stepped outside for a moment without you knowing it?'

'Sure they could.' Abruptly, Maggie rose. 'Come on.'

She led the way to the back of the bar, around a corner into a narrow tiled corridor. A door marked WOMEN was directly across from the back door of the Nightwood Bar.

'Anybody who went to the john could've gone out there. I know you aren't going to ask me who went to the john.'

Kate smiled; she had been about to ask.

Maggie lit another Pall Mall, unzipping one of her innumerable pockets and stuffing the match into it. She gestured toward the door. 'She's still out there, isn't she? Dory.'

'It takes time,' Kate said softly. 'We mean no disrespect, believe me when I tell you that. We have to be extremely careful because if we make mistakes now, we can never recover from them. We'll be calling the deputy coroner soon to come for her.'

'I understand,' Maggie said, walking back toward their table. 'It's just that . . . The poor kid. . . .'

Kate sat down and picked up her coffee mug, thinking that lying out in the cool night air was the least of the indignities yet to be suffered by the body of Dory Quillin. She asked, 'What can you tell us about her? How did she support herself and her van?'

Maggie shrugged and flicked ash from her cigarette with a scarred thumbnail. 'I make it a point not to know what my customers do for a living. After twenty years in this business you learn to listen to what customers want to tell you, you learn to be careful about asking questions – even in the areas they talk about.'

'But you know she has parents,' Kate pressed, sensing evasion. 'They live here locally, right? How did you know that?'

'She talked about them. Nothing in any detail, just bitter remarks.'

'Like what? What did she say?'

'I don't really remember. What you'd expect in her circumstances – that they weren't into what she was about . . . I honestly don't remember.'

Taylor asked, 'Why did they kick her out? How could they let a girl like her go live in a van?'

What a perfectly stupid question, Kate thought, waiting for Maggie to answer it.

'Why did they kick her out,' Maggie repeated. Her hooded dark eyes were cold. 'Detective Taylor, take a survey in any gay bar. One hell of a lot of us were kicked out by our families. My own parents decided that nothing could be worse than having a gay daughter.'

'Well, I know that goes on,' Taylor blustered, 'we see all kinds of kids in the street – but God to look at her it's still hard to figure . . . I don't see how anybody could just. . . .'

My own parents, Kate thought, how would they have reacted? She had never risked telling them – and now death had taken them beyond her reach.

'What about romantic liaisons?' Kate asked, interrupting Taylor's floundering. 'Was she involved with anybody here?'

Maggie rolled her eyes. 'You can't expect me to answer a question like that. I don't know what goes on with all these women – you might as well ask me to keep track of what's happening in a rabbit hutch.'

Kate and Taylor chuckled. Kate said, 'Then to your knowledge there was no one in particular, is that correct?'

Maggie shifted in her chair. 'Well . . . I think maybe there was somebody a while back.' She shrugged. 'Dory went for older women, she never seemed interested in the younger ones, and a lot of young women were after her. I think she'd have even made a play for these ancient bones if I'd given her any indication.'

'And you didn't?' Taylor said, looking at her intently.

Maggie stared back at him. 'If I wanted children, I'd be a heterosexual.'

Taylor chuckled uncertainly and went back to his notes.

'The baseball game today,' Kate said. 'Did Dory play?'

'Second base. Batted lead-off.'

'Did you play too?'

'Are you kidding? I show up once in a while, it's fun to watch the kids. Pickup teams from the other bars get together, we have a game every now and again.'

'These women from the other bars,' Taylor interjected, 'did you notice Dory talking with anybody? Maybe leave with someone?'

Maggie shook her head. 'Too young for her, all of them. As I remember, I don't think she even knew that many to talk to. And they were all gone before we left the park.'

Kate asked, 'Did she act . . . different in any way? Say anything unusual?'

Maggie leaned her chin on a hand, her eyes almost closing as she reflected. 'Well . . . she always was a little hyper . . . and she was like that today too, maybe a little more so. She'd just come back from a day or so out of town –'

'Where?' Kate and Taylor asked simultaneously.

Maggie looked startled. 'Central California somewhere – I don't remember where. Hell, I wasn't paying any attention. I mean, I didn't care – you think it might be important?'

Kate said, 'Right now we have to assume everything's important.'

'What can you tell us about the women here?' Taylor asked.

Maggie stubbed out her cigarette. 'About as much as I could tell you about Dory.'

Kate heard the wariness and took an indirect approach. 'Would you identify everyone for us? Which ones were at the park?'

'Patton was there.' Maggie smiled at Kate. 'Of course you know who Patton is.'

Kate grinned back. 'The one with the extreme opinions.'

'Extreme, you say. She thinks I'm corrupting the bodily temples of my sisters by serving them alcohol. She has lots of other free advice and opinions too – like I should share with my sisters any money I make beyond what it costs me to subsist.' Maggie's chuckle was humorless. 'No problem there – I make just enough to get by.'

Taylor glanced over at Patton who was leaning across the bar gesturing with both hands as she talked to Roz. 'If this was my bar,' he said, 'she wouldn't get one foot in the door.'

'A distinct temptation,' Maggie admitted. 'She's a real pain. But I always remember that firebrand women like her are the ones who've made everything happen in women's rights.'

'So who else was at the park,' Taylor said uninterestedly, returning to his notes.

'The Latina in the red baseball shirt – she's Tora. The other Latina sitting next to Patton is Ash – Ash was here at the bar. Kendall was at the park, she's the one in chino pants and the white polo shirt. And so was Raney, she's the black woman with the Grace Jones haircut. The other black woman was here, her name is Audie.'

'Where do they get such names,' Kate grumbled, writing rapidly.

'What's your first name?'

'Kate.'

'Ever wanted to change it?'

'It never occurred to me.' She was writing brief descriptions of the women at the bar to go with each name.

'Let's say you've broken away from a religion you absolutely despise,' Maggie said. 'And let's say your parents have named you Bernadette Theresa after their two favorite saints.'

Kate smiled. 'I see what you mean.'

'That's only one reason some of these women choose their own names.'

'The woman at the end of the bar,' Kate said. 'You didn't mention her.'

'Don't know her. She was here, not at the park. She's been coming in a lot, but too recently to call her a regular.'

'When did she start coming in?'

'Maybe two weeks ago.'

Kate looked at the woman with interest. 'These other women – they're regulars?'

Maggie nodded. 'Some come in more than others, but I see all of them at least a couple of times a week.'

Taylor said, 'You're certain you never saw this woman before two weeks ago?'

'Positive. I'd remember. Who wouldn't?'

The woman, wearing earth-toned pants and a huge, shapeless tan shirt, was in three-quarter profile to Kate, listening to Patton. Her large eyes were almond-shaped, her forehead high; her dark hair was pulled up under a close-fitting beige cap of metallic-threaded fabric. The small lips were full, the cheekbones fully fleshed; her skin had the high orange duskiness of a complex racial mixture. She reminded Kate of statues depicting queens of ancient Egypt.

'Exotic,' Taylor commented to Maggie. 'Know anything about her?'

'Second week she came in, Audie approached her. Audie's the most kind-hearted soul . . . Anyway, all Audie said was, cheer up, honey, nothing's that bad – something like that. For her trouble she got stared right into the floor. Miss Deep Freeze, that's what I call her.'

Amused, Kate studied Miss Deep Freeze, who sat one stool over from Kendall, looking weary and bored.

'Lover trouble,' Maggie said. 'No other reason a woman like her starts coming in here. If you're with somebody, or if you're by yourself and you feel okay about it, you don't have to be in a women's bar for hours every single night of the week.'

Taylor said, 'Your neighbors – the motel, the businesses down the hill, how do they feel about you being here? Any trouble with them?'

Good question, Kate thought. A neighborhood canvass just might furnish some good leads. . . .

Maggie shook her head. 'At first. They're still not exactly overjoyed to have us. But the place isn't that noisy, even on Saturday nights. Sure we have a jukebox, but I won't have loud music or loud women.' She looked sharply at Kate. 'You think somebody did this because . . . You think some gang maybe wandered up here and did this . . . for kicks?'

'Maggie, we don't know,' Kate said earnestly. 'We haven't even formed a theory yet. We solve most homicides because most people are killed by people they know. But random violence *is* a possibility – it's an increasing problem everywhere.'

Maggie's dark eyes were fixed on hers. 'I've been here four good years. I wanted this bar to be a good quiet place, I've never advertised, just depended on word of mouth. I've never made waves, never had to call the cops, never once had trouble. Well,' she amended, 'no trouble we couldn't handle ourselves. Everybody who comes here wants to keep this place something special, without any cops involved. We never let anything get out of hand. . . .' Maggie drained her coffee. 'Publicity,' she hissed. 'Now the nuts'll know we're here . . .'

Publicity, Kate knew, would be a few lines in the *Times*, perhaps a paragraph in the *Herald Examiner* – the life snuffed out here deemed insufficiently important for more. 'We'll do everything we can – you have my word on that. Would you give my partner and me a few minutes? Then we'll talk to Patton.'

'Sure.' Maggie rose, tucking in the tail of her T-shirt. 'Take care of the tough one first, right?'

'Right,' Kate answered with a smile.

Kate had made the judgment that because of Patton's belligerence, the best strategy was to interview her first; if she could not be turned into a cooperative witness then they would dismiss her, get her off the premises. The stack of FI's compiled by Hansen and his men contained drivers' license numbers and the legal names of these women, no matter what they preferred to call themselves – and also their addresses. If she and Taylor developed information requiring a follow-up interview, they would be able to find Patton. . . .

As Maggie returned to the bar, Kate's measuring gaze followed her. Taylor asked, 'How do you peg her?'

'Cautious, close-mouthed, too careful about what she said to us. I think we'll have to move inch by inch with her, maybe with all these women. What do you think?'

'Me? I think this bar, this whole scene is weird, Kate. Up here out of the way . . . You come to a bar to drink and socialize, for chrissakes, not to play chess or read *Playboy*.'

Kate chuckled, knowing Taylor expected appreciation of his wit, knowing he could never understand that to her this bar felt right and natural and good in every respect. He could never imagine the relief of escaping the claustrophobic heterosexual world into a secluded, private place where there were only other lesbians. . .

Taylor continued, 'I think what our bartender Maggie suggested is a good possible. One or more thugs wandered up here and bashed her head in just for the hell of it.'

Hating such a possibility and the slender odds of finding such a killer, Kate shrugged. 'It's as likely as anything else,' she conceded. 'Let's talk with sweet, friendly Patton.'

At Taylor's call of her name, Patton jerked around to stare at them, her body stiffening.

'What do you bet,' Taylor said to Kate, 'she won't come over here.'

'And miss a chance to sneer at us? Sure she'll come over.'

Patton unhooked a pair of aviator sunglasses from the pocket of her shirt and put them on, picked up a cigarette from an ashtray on the bar and put it in her mouth. Stuffing her hands in the pockets of her cutoffs, she slid from her bar stool, and sauntered over. She kicked away the fourth chair at Kate's table, and with the same foot pushed the remaining chair equidistant between Kate and Taylor. Not taking her hands from her pockets she eased herself into the chair and crossed an ankle over a knee. Smoke rising from the cigarette in the corner of her mouth, she looked at Kate through her mirrored glasses.

Kate asked flatly, 'What can you tell us about the young woman lying dead out there?'

'Nothing.' Ashes spilled down the front of Patton's blue-checked shirt. Her sunglasses glinted in the barroom light.

'How long have you known her?'

Patton looked up at the ceiling for some moments. 'Maybe a year,' she said.

Kate sat back and studied her unhurriedly, examining the cropped blonde hair visible under the yacht cap, the thin sharp features, the tight white line of her mouth. The Adidas jogging shoe Patton had propped on a knee began a cadenced beat, as if to a rhythm she heard in her head. Kate said, 'What time did you arrive here from the park?'

'Same time as everybody else,' Patton muttered from around her cigarette, the jogging shoe increasing its beat.

'What time was that?'

Patton shrugged.

'We don't understand shrugs,' Kate said evenly. 'Are you telling us that you won't answer or that you don't know?'

Patton grinned, removed a hand from a pocket, took the cigarette from her mouth. 'I don't know.'

'Did you notice anything unusual, either at the park or here afterward?'

Patton shrugged. As Kate's stare froze on her, she grinned again. 'I don't know,' she said.

Taylor spoke. 'Do you have any idea what Dory Quillin did for a living?'

'She was a nuclear physicist,' Patton said.

Kate and Taylor looked at her silently.

'Maybe I should spell that for you,' Patton said. 'N-u-c —'

'Patton,' Kate said, closing her notebook, 'we're making an honest effort to find out who took a very young woman's life.' She pulled a card from the notebook and placed it in front of Patton. 'When you're finished with all this posturing, when you realize that what's happened here tonight is just a little more important than you think you are, call us.'

Patton sat looking at Kate, her masked eyes invisible, her mouth impassive.

'Now get out of here,' Kate said.

'You have no right to order me around.'

'This bar is part of an official crime scene. And in any case it's hardly open for business. I'll be glad to have an officer escort you.'

'I just bet you would.' Patton rose. Ignoring Kate's card,

she turned her back on the detectives and marched back to the bar.

'Nice going,' Taylor commented. 'Myself, I was considering police brutality.'

Kate smiled thinly. 'Ed, I don't see any reason not to notify the coroner.'

'Me neither. Let me take care of it, Kate. Why don't I work out there with Hansen? You might work better solo in here.'

'I doubt it but go ahead,' Kate said. 'They don't like me much either.'

'Maybe not, but this being a women's bar . . . I feel some extra vibrations, myself.'

Taylor's masculine presence in this bar, Kate thought, was a fact she resented as much as any woman here.

Taylor pulled himself to his feet and walked to the door of the Nightwood Bar. Patton followed, dragging a jogging shoe over the path Taylor took, stomping and scraping, as if to erase each of his footsteps. 'A man!' she shouted. 'In our bar! Yechhh!'

As Taylor stopped to look back at Kate, shaking his head, Patton leaned over and whispered to him. Adjusting his tie, again shaking his head, he exited from the Nightwood Bar.

Patton polished the doorknob with her sleeve. 'Yechhh,' she uttered once again, then opened the door and vanished into the night.

CHAPTER 3

Kate called Tora over to the table. The Chicana sat with her chair pulled back, arms folded across her red baseball shirt, her legs crossed so tightly the ankles were wrapped around each other. She watched Kate with resentful brown eyes. No, she didn't know Dory Quillin very well. No, she hadn't noticed anything unusual at the ballpark. Yes, she had arrived at the bar around five-thirty, along with everyone else. No, she had not seen or heard anything unusual. No, she had nothing more to add about Dory Quillin or why this had happened.

Kate remembered Harry Johnstone, a grizzled sergeant who had befriended her when she first started her police career. 'Thirty years a cop,' he had muttered to her at his retirement party, an arm heavily around her shoulders, his eyes red-rimmed with drink and the finality of leave-taking. 'For what? For shit. The fucking people hate us. They like us when they need us. Otherwise they fucking want us out of their face.'

More than most she understood that instinctive recoil from the uniformed figure with a badge and a gun. It was not so much the sanctified authority to kill or maim but the power to subvert, to diminish and scar a life. Implicit in that power to arrest was the potential to exercise it for capricious, cruel, or even thoughtless ends. Small wonder that the cop was the personification of menace to many gay people already brutalized by contempt, whose lives testified to powerlessness without recourse.

One after another Kate called the patrons of the Nightwood Bar. Kendall's hostility was no less obvious than

26

Patton's, but less overt. Ash was as close-mouthed as Tora, curt and impatient with Kate's questions. Audie was not hostile but neither was she cooperative – she would not meet Kate's eyes. Roz was so genuinely bewildered by the evening's events that Kate dismissed her after a few perfunctory questions.

Kate looked over her notes. With one woman remaining to be interviewed, she had learned nothing useful about Dory Quillin or why she had died. Kate accepted a fourth cup of coffee from Maggie, and remembered her first visit to a lesbian bar.

It had been Julie's idea to drive from Ann Arbor to Detroit that Saturday night – Kate's twenty-first birthday. Kate could not afterward recall the name of the bar, only that it was in the vicinity of downtown, amid a war zone of defaced, scarred, graffiti-sprayed buildings.

The bartender, wearing army fatigues, her hair in a brushcut, had been so masculine that Kate would never have questioned her gender except in these circumstances. Other women in that bar were equally masculine – some clad in jackets and ties and wing-tipped shoes. They sat with frilly women who wore low-cut blouses and mini-skirts and spike heels, gaudy jewelry and lacquered hairdos and bright lipstick with matching nails.

Sitting with Julie at a corner table in the dim smoky room, Kate added her own nervous smoke to the haze, and watched figures sway on the dance floor to the songs of Patti Page, Connie Francis, Jo Stafford, the Everly Brothers – as if this bar, in 1967, had been caught and held in the rose-hued romanticism of the fifties.

The masculine bartender circulated with a large tray of drinks, serving a fresh scotch and soda to Kate, a daiquiri to Julie. 'From her,' she said, and jerked her head toward a blonde young woman sitting at the bar in knee-high boots, a leather mini-skirt, a fringed buckskin vest.

As Kate made a gesture of refusal the bartender growled, 'Relax, okay? She's a hooker. They come in sometimes, they like to toss their money around on women.'

Kate accepted her drink, and became absorbed in watching

the woman. She had come in alone, and now sat with her back against the railing of the bar, surveying the room. She was soon approached by a dark-haired boyish woman in slacks and a shirt. Kate watched them dance through five songs, their steps and tempo the same regardless of the beat – slow, and increasingly sinuous. The women left together, the boyish woman's arm around the other's waist. Kate stared at the barroom door long after they had disappeared through it.

To meet a stranger, and not half an hour later to leave with that stranger and take her to bed . . . Kate savored the last of her paid-for-drink as if it were rare nectar never again to be tasted. The woman who had bought it existed in a world whose parameters Kate could not fathom.

She and Julie stayed on, drinking, watching other women drink and dance and play pool. Other people also sat and watched, couples – straight men and women – avidly staring. Kate felt inchoate anger – and humiliation.

Her curt rejection of Julie's wish to dance was a refusal to be part of a freak show for these voyeurs. This place, charged as it was with music and noisy conversation and activity, was too much like the place which housed her grandmother – a ghetto of the exiled, of the classified hopeless.

Several of the masculine women, requesting Kate's permission asked Julie to dance. Kate watched Julie in their arms without resentment or jealousy or emotion of any kind, wondering at her own passivity and emptiness, and why it seemed so suddenly obvious that her life had always been like a compass without direction.

The next weekend when Julie again wanted to leave campus and return to the bar, Kate refused with granite finality. 'Then I'll go by myself,' Julie had declared.

Soon Julie was gone from the University of Michigan and from Kate's life, captured by one of the women in that Detroit bar.

In her last year of college Kate had listened to a Marine Corps recruiter who ventured on campus in the teeth of the Vietnam uproar. She understood only in retrospect that enlistment was her own protest – her first significant defiance of a peer group which had dictated too many aspects of her life. And four years later she had met Anne – and in the precious years afterward her life had expanded in meaning and impact. Never again had she set foot in a lesbian bar. . . .

Kate looked up from her notes and beckoned to the last remaining patron in the Nightwood Bar.

The woman Maggie had called Miss Deep Freeze took a seat opposite Kate. Under the lights, close up, her dusky skin acquired glossiness and an umber tone. She looked at Kate with remote, wounded dark eyes. Her beauty contained a poignance that touched Kate in an interior place as she remembered Maggie's speculation about 'lover trouble.' She herself shared with this woman a similar loss – she too had been deserted, abandoned to life by the precious lover who had left her for death. . . .

'May I ask why you're staring at me?'

Kate started. 'I'm sorry. Could I risk offending you further and ask your racial origin?'

Miss Deep Freeze did not change expression. 'Most people don't ask – they just stare. Spanish and Jamaican on one side, English and Japanese on the other.'

Kate nodded. 'I thought it was perhaps something like that. You make me think that in a totally integrated world we would all be very beautiful.'

The woman smiled, her teeth strong and even. The faint scent of musk reached Kate.

Kate asked, 'What's your name?'

'Andrea Ross.'

All that ethnicity and a simple American name – it was almost comical. Kate returned her smile and said, 'Finally, someone with a last name.'

'It's simple paranoia, you know.' The voice was low and musical, from deep in the throat. Andrea Ross gestured with graceful fingers toward the bar, as if the women Kate had dismissed were still sitting there. 'They think they've come out because they're at a lesbian bar. But they're scared like all of us. They still want to control who identifies them, they don't want to be exposed on their jobs or to their families or whatever. And they sure don't want to be involved in this.'

'You don't seem worried.'

'I'm sure I should be.' Andrea Ross pushed up the sleeves of her oversize shirt and picked up her drink, a screwdriver.

'What do you do for a living, Miss Ross?'

'Miss Ross sells real estate.' She sipped her drink, the small full lips curving upward before they touched the rim of the glass.

Kate smiled again. 'I'm sure Miss Ross does very well.'

'Not spectacularly well, but she manages to get the bills paid. Is the detective ready to drink something stronger than coffee at this late hour?'

'Not while she's on duty,' Kate replied, quite willing to play the game. 'She thanks you for the consideration.' She added, 'You're refreshingly non-defensive compared to the other women here.'

Andrea said somberly, 'I've listened to them complain about their lives, the way the world treats them. The way I see it, this world may be rotten but it's the only one we have and I can't see how anyone can hope to make a difference by trying to leave it. But that's what Patton and these women mostly talk about when they talk their politics – they dream of separation.'

Andrea was speaking easily, in an assumption of understanding. Kate wondered if her statements were cooperation with the police or simply conversation with another lesbian. Again remembering Maggie's assessment of the woman sitting before her, Kate chose her next words carefully. 'Still, you give the impression of being somewhat . . . bitter.'

Andrea shrugged. 'You can be bitter about things that have nothing to do with gay politics.'

The statement, the flat tone of the voice, did not invite further comment or question. 'Dory Quillin,' Kate said. Now that she had established rapport, however tenuous, she redirected the conversation. 'Did you know her?'

'I knew her by name, by sight, by reputation. She came on to me once. After that she said hello to me. By your definition, did I know her?'

Kate looked down at her notes. This woman was stylish, intriguing, disturbing. 'You knew her by sight. What were your impressions?'

'A heartbreakingly beautiful child.'

'Who came on to you,' Kate said, hardening her tone.

'This particular beautiful child was desperately needy, very troubled, totally messed up. I didn't need a psychiatrist's report – those things were very obvious to me. I'm only thirty-three, but just the thought of all that neediness in bed quite frankly exhausted me.'

Kate chuckled. Andrea looked at her expressionlessly, then took a sip of her drink. She said, 'She fascinated all the women here. But they were leery of her, there was something too reckless in her. They speculated about her all the time, wild things –'

'What wild things?'

'Drugs, women, men, Mafia, orgies – whatever their minds could conjure up. Dory didn't belong here. Most kids her age hang out at Peanuts or the Palm, or the bars in the Valley. Obviously she was looking for something else. A mother-lover.'

Andrea looked away from Kate and continued in a tired voice, 'Gay women like to think we have more enlightened attitudes about age difference in our relationships. But I suspect sometimes we're just trying to get back to a safer time when we were our mothers' daughters. Back to when we were children and had no knowledge of men and how much they would control our lives.'

Kate nodded, willing to sit there as long as Andrea Ross was willing to talk.

'The women in here use alcohol but not illegal chemicals – they disapprove of them. They're down on what they don't understand, anything they're half-scared of. They're too far removed from someone like Dory Quillin.'

Kate asked casually, 'Was Dory Quillin into drugs?'

'Isn't everybody?'

Kate waited.

After several moments Andrea said, 'Let me put it this way. She asked me to come back to her van, she offered me some coke if it was to my liking. I don't think she was talking about the stuff in cans.'

'And you didn't go?' Kate prompted.

'I wasn't into her and I don't do drugs. Which has nothing

to do with generation gaps or virtue. My brother OD'd when he was seventeen.'

'I'm sorry,' Kate offered.

Andrea's shrug was a habitual gesture, Kate saw, a method of temporizing until she gathered her thoughts. 'Tony was trying to find a way to kill himself from the time he was ten – I'll never know why.'

Kate studied her. 'You had the same feeling about Dory Quillin? Is that why you avoided her?'

Her eyes distant, Andrea turned her glass slowly in slender fingers. 'I felt inadequate, that's why I avoided her. I'd have felt that way about anyone. Right now I need everything about myself for myself.'

Her eyes cleared; she looked at Kate with a directness Kate found disconcerting. 'I never thought she was self-destructive. Exactly the opposite. There seemed to be something very healthy in her, struggling to get out.'

Kate made a note of the assessment, finding it both comforting and saddening. 'I know you've been coming here only two weeks –' She broke off as Andrea raised both eyebrows. 'One of the women told me. Any investigation is made possible only because half the world gossips about the other half.' She phrased her question with care: 'Do you happen to know if any of these women here tonight was involved with Dory in more than a casual way?'

'Patton.'

Kate heard this with disappointment, then a stirring of surprise. 'Patton,' she said, her mind filled with the image of the blonde child in the parking lot. She murmured, 'It seems such . . . an odd pairing. To me.'

'From the way the other women teased Patton about it, apparently it was very brief. My guess is, she took Dory on as an indoctrination project – Patton's just the type. I know some youngsters Dory's age are susceptible, but I can't see her being much interested in political rhetoric. To me her needs seemed much more basic. . . .' Andrea drained her drink and set the glass down with finality.

Kate could think of no other questions for Andrea Ross, other than personal ones that were inappropriate. She said, 'I appreciate your help.'

'One more thing,' Andrea said. 'Someone was in here maybe two weeks ago, early evening. A black woman, fortyish. I heard the women call her Neely, they talked about her when she left. She was Dory's lover for a while – I don't know for how long.'

'Was she looking for Dory?'

'I don't know. I understand she used to come in all the time, but not after Dory was staying here.'

'Thank you.' Kate handed Andrea one of her cards.

Andrea turned the card in her fingers. 'Detective Kate Delafield,' she said. 'So you'd like me to call you.'

She did not look at Kate; the meaning was clear in her voice.

If you think of anything more to tell me about this case, was what Kate must tell her, was required to tell her. Instead she answered, 'Yes'.

CHAPTER 4

Kate drove up La Brea toward West Hollywood, Taylor beside her. The familiar street was silent and deserted at this hour on a Sunday night except for a few cars in clusters dictated by traffic lights. She focused on the street instead of the coming task: notifying the Quillin family of the homicide of their daughter.

She glanced at Robaire's, a French restaurant between Beverly and Wilshire, incongruous amid the fluttering flags of new and used car lots and auto supply houses and a supermarket. She had not, she realized, had dinner. Above Beverly she watched the street steadily improve into tidy graphics shops, film businesses, a ballet school – except for one dilapidated remainder of days past: Pink's, a hotdog stand to which Taylor had once lured her, proclaiming it the best in the city and a historical landmark as well. Kate remembered a historical attack of indigestion.

As they approached Santa Monica Boulevard, Kate's thoughts returned to the women of the Nightwood Bar. 'By the way,' she said to Taylor, 'what did Patton say to you at the door?'

'Nothing much.' Then Taylor growled, 'What the hell is a patriarchal pig?'

Kate laughed.

'Gimme a break, Kate.'

'Look it up in the dictionary, Ed.'

The intersection they approached was not unusual – a Carl's Jr. on one corner, a Thrifty Drug across from it, a carwash on another corner, a McDonald's just a little further

34

up the block – except for the blue sign which announced: WEST HOLLYWOOD.

Kate had not been here since the election in November when the area had incorporated itself; this intersection now formed a boundary of the most unusual new city in America, with three gay members elected to its five-person city council, one of them now serving as the mayor *pro tem*.

She turned onto Santa Monica Boulevard. At eleven o'clock this Sunday night considerable pedestrian traffic moved along each side of the street, mostly men strolling in pairs. Beside her, Taylor shifted his buttocks, his head raised and alert as if he were inhaling new and somewhat suspect air.

'One more year,' he muttered. 'Then Marie and me, we're moving our butts out of this goddam looney bin of a town.'

'Orange County, I presume.'

'Further on down toward San Diego,' Taylor answered, missing her sarcasm as she knew he would. 'Maybe I'll learn to play golf. Grow avocados.'

'Exciting, Ed.'

'Shit on excitement.'

Kate did not answer. They had reached Holloway Drive and she was looking out at the median strip dividing Santa Monica Boulevard. She peered ahead as far as she could see. Flagpoles, perhaps twenty feet high and set perhaps the same distance apart, held small flags, each of a different nation, each whipping smartly in the late night breeze. She was moved by these vestiges of last summer's Olympic games, and the memory of those few exalted days when the sun-splashed city had seemed cleaner, brighter, more glistening than usual, when classic athletes from around the globe had symbolized the best in the human species and had made her briefly forget the dark side she constantly saw. . . .

They passed the Sheriff's Station on San Vicente, still the law enforcement agency for West Hollywood; then restaurants and nightclubs: Dan Tana's, La Masia, the Troubadour. 'We're almost to Beverly Hills,' Kate grumbled. 'Where *is* this place?'

'Turn right on Doheny,' Taylor said, consulting the map. 'Christ, listen to these street names, Kate. Harland, Keith,

Lloyd – this city, even the streets have boys' names. Jesus, here's one called Dicks.'

'Gay or straight, the whole world discriminates against women,' Kate said good-humoredly. She was looking at the large dark shapes of apartment buildings along Doheny and across at a row of royal palms, craning to see the majestic height of them; but their tops were invisible in the darkness.

'Turn right,' Taylor ordered.

Kate cruised slowly down the block. Hemmed in by the large buildings on Doheny and the commerce on Santa Monica, the well-lighted neighborhood was a labyrinth of streets so narrow that parking was allowed on one side only. All the houses were small and of individual design, many Spanish style, most with barred windows. All were built forward on their lots, leaving miniscule patches of lawn, some fenced in with low stone barriers. Shrubbery was scarce – a few low trees, some carefully sculptured bushes. The small houses and narrow streets reminded Kate of Venice on her own side of town.

The windows of the Quillin house were entirely barred, including a side window a five-year-old child could not wriggle through. The foundation of the house and the sidewalk leading to the street were lined with rose bushes, their blooms in various stages of fullness and decay; as Kate made her way along the pathway of roses she saw an assortment of plastic ducks reposing on the loam between the bushes.

'Planning on a few ducks among your avocado trees?' Kate joked through a clenched jaw. She had glanced in the barred front window at a scene of domestic peace – a husband and wife watching the eleven o'clock news.

'Naw, maybe a few chickens.' Taylor pressed the doorbell, stood back, smoothed his jacket, inhaled an audible breath. Kate was aware of the sweet scent of roses amid the faint metallic smell of smog.

'Who is it?' The voice was high-pitched, tremulous.

'Police, ma'am,' Taylor answered. 'If you'll step to your front window we'll be glad to show you identification.'

Kate heard the rasp of a safety chain. The woman who opened the front door was fiftyish, her body's thin shapelessness clad in a yellow cotton dress. Her washed-out blue eyes fixed themselves on Kate.

Kate extended her badge and ID. 'Detective Delafield, Los Angeles Police Department. This is my partner, Detective Taylor. May we come in, please?'

The woman's hand went to her throat. It was the veined hand of a seventy-year-old.

'God yes, come in,' said the barrel-chested man who had come up behind her; he wore a green plaid bathrobe. 'Let's not let the whole neighborhood in on this, whatever it is.'

Kate and Taylor walked into the living room. Taylor asked, 'May we sit down?' He took a chair without waiting for a reply. Kate sat in an armchair across from him.

'It's about Dolores,' the woman said, sinking heavily into the sofa. The man looked toward a corduroy-covered recliner, then sat down beside her.

Kate cleared her throat. 'You're the parents of Dolores Marie Quillin?'

'I'm Roland Quillin, this is my wife Flora.' He leaned toward them, his shoulders slumped. 'What has she done now?'

'We're sorry to have to inform you,' Kate said evenly, 'that she was killed early this evening.'

Roland Quillin reached for his wife's hand; husband and wife stared at each other.

'I'm truly sorry,' Kate added in the same even voice.

'My condolences to both you folks,' Taylor said solemnly.

Kate felt her familiar sensation of wishing she could be anywhere on earth except where she was. She had delivered similar messages in her thirteen years in police work, and always her feeling was the same: that she was an intruder on the most private, the most sacred of emotions. That day a year and ten months ago when she was informed in the Captain's office at Wilshire Division of Anne's death, she herself had craved only solitude, to be in a dark cave in some faraway place, to curl her pain-wracked body into a tight ball. . . .

'Roland . . .'

Flora Quillin's mouth worked, almost with a life of its

own – a small mouth with a delicacy Dory Quillin had inherited, and apparently all she had inherited.

Kate stared at lank, chemically uniform blonde hair, at pallid skin pulled tightly over a thin-featured face, at raw-boned arms, at the nondescript yellow dress, at canvas espadrilles on bare, blue-veined feet. Flora Quillin seemed an especially cruel caricature of her daughter.

'Flora, we knew it would happen . . . God we *knew* it. . . .'

Roland Quillin's eyes had slowly widened until the whites showed all around the irises. They were blue eyes, deeper blue than either his wife's or his daughter's. In his early sixties, he was nearly bald, with a shapeless nose and deep creases around his eyes. A barely perceptible scar lay along a freshly shaven cheekbone, the scar slightly curved, one a knife slash might have made years ago, Kate thought. Irritation from the recent shaving had probably given it this much visibility.

She was momentarily disconcerted when Roland Quillin's eyes suddenly intercepted hers, interrupting her concentrated scrutiny of him.

He said slowly, distinctly, 'Dolores hasn't been a daughter to us for a long time.'

She's dead, Kate wanted to scream at him, your daughter's *dead!* How could anything else matter now? Three-quarters of her life had been taken away. . . .

Taylor spoke: 'May we ask why that happened, sir?'

Roland Quillin crossed his arms across the plaid robe. 'Check your records at LAPD,' he said flatly.

Again he looked at his wife, who stared back at him. 'Flora,' he said softly, 'it's a blessing. It's God will.'

Kate said quietly, 'Mr Quillin, we know these are painful circumstances. But we'd appreciate knowing what we'll find.'

Roland Quillin's arms tightened across his chest.

Andrea Ross had mentioned cocaine, Kate mused, watching his thin mouth pinch downward. Perhaps Dory Quillin had gotten into serious trouble with drugs.

'Prostitution,' he said.

Assimilating this new information, Kate sat back in her armchair, rubbing her hands along its smooth fabric, angry with herself at her shock. She was too experienced in police work – and too old for God's sake – to be deceived by the white-clad innocence of that young body, those bewildered silver-blue eyes. She felt unreasoning anger at Dory Quillin. That face in death had conveyed betrayal. She herself now felt betrayed.

Taylor said, 'Sounds like she was quite a trial for you folks.'

Kate added a nod of agreement. Taylor's sympathetic tone and approach, regardless of its genuiness, was effective police procedure.

Roland Quillin asked, 'What happened to her?'

Not trusting the tact of Taylor's reply, Kate answered, 'It appears that it was a single blow of . . . a blunt instrument.'

Flora Quillin asked in a tremulous voice, 'Do you think she . . . suffered?'

'I don't believe so,' Kate said gently, pitying her. Who could ever know what Dory Quillin had felt? 'We received the initial report around six o'clock. Our best estimate is that she was . . . deceased shortly before that time.'

Roland Quillin asked in a tone of intense bitterness, 'Was it one of her *customers*? Or one of her female . . . *companions?*'

Kate said, 'Sir, at this point we're still piecing our information together.'

Taylor opened his notebook. 'We do need an official identification, we'll need one or both of you to –'

'No,' Roland Quillin said.

'Sir?' Taylor looked up in surprise.

'No,' he repeated. 'We don't want to see her.'

'Mrs. Quillin –' Kate began.

'I couldn't bear to look at her.' The words were uttered in a whisper.

Kate exchanged a glance with Taylor, who raised an eyebrow almost imperceptibly. Agonized by what she was witnessing in this room, she said quietly, 'You had her fairly late in life, Mrs Quillin.'

'I was thirty-five, yes.'

The voice was soft, the words slightly inflected. Southern, Kate guessed. Maybe Texas. She asked, 'Do you have other children?'

'Just her. I wasn't the same after that, never quite well, I'm still not well, you know ... And she was a colicky child, trouble, she was so much trouble. More and more trouble, she was such a rebel, she was sick in her head, she ...' She looked helplessly at Kate, then at her husband.

'Ran off at fourteen,' he said. 'Gone two weeks the first time. You people found her in Hollywood. *Arrested* her. In one of those ... *motels*.' He added, 'We took her back — that time.' He raised his hands in a gesture of futility.

'Fourteen, only fourteen she was,' Flora Quillin said. 'What did she know about anything? She was sick in her head by then. But she always claimed to know everything. From the time she was ten. Full of the wildest tales, you never knew when she was telling the truth about anything. Why one time she —'

'She left twice more,' Roland Quillin cut in. 'Wouldn't tell us what she'd been doing after she decided to come back home. But all that money she had, we knew. Sixteen years old, wild as a coyote. ...'

Kate said in a soft tone, 'From what you said earlier, Mr. Quillin, you also knew your daughter was a lesbian.'

'That was the last straw,' Roland Quillin told them. 'Not bad enough she had to turn herself into a common streetwalker —'

Flora Quillin asked, 'Could I perhaps get you detectives something to drink? There's coffee already made ...'

'Appreciate it,' Taylor said. 'Black, please.' Kate shook her head no. She could not eat or drink anything in this house.

Kate's eyes followed Flora Quillin, and then took in the room — a room reminiscent of her own growing up and the houses of childhood friends she had not thought of in years. The sofa and matching armchairs were of bright floral chintz, the coffee table and end tables of maple, with the blockiness of early-American furniture popular during the fifties. Over the corduroy-covered recliner an ornate green lampshade hung from a hook; the room's other two lamps had bases of milk glass, and fluted shades. Beige shag carpeting was protected by area rugs in front of the sofa, the recliner, and led from the living room into the other rooms of the house. A maple hutch, visible in the dining room, was crammed with dishes and knick-knacks. A sewing bag on a maple dining room chair spilled out knitting in shades of red. On the far wall of the dining room a cross hung next to a small framed reproduction of St. Francis feeding the birds.

Flora Quillin handed a steaming mug of coffee to Taylor, and placed a coaster on the coffee table. Taylor set the mug carefully on the coaster.

Kate asked, 'How long has it been since you . . . gave up on your daughter?'

'Two years ago?' Roland Quillin inquired of his wife. 'Was that when she brought home that . . . that . . . and told us they were . . .'

'The woman was *black*.' Flora Quillin said to Kate. 'Twenty years *older* than Dolores and *black besides*. It was nearly the death of us. Everything, that sick child did *everything* to humilate and hurt us, it was like she stayed up *nights* thinking of ways.'

'I can see that she was a trial to you,' Kate said. 'How old was she by then?'

'Seventeen.'

Four hours ago when she died Dory Quillin had been nineteen years old. . . .

'Where,' Roland Quillin asked wearily, 'did this happen?'

Kate replied, 'Her body was found in a parking lot on La Brea. Behind a place called the Nightwood Bar.'

'The Nightwood Bar,' Roland Quillin repeated. He rubbed his face with both hands. 'She even had to die at a lesbian bar.'

Flora Quillin asked in a quavering voice, 'Will all this be in the papers?'

'We don't know ma'am,' Taylor answered. 'Too hard to predict what the L.A. papers will decide to cover. We have homicides in the city every day – some never get in the papers at all.'

'We've lived in this house over twenty years,' Flora Quillin declared. 'You can't imagine what it's been like having everyone *know* about Dolores. To have all those people *pity* you because your only child –'

Kate asked, 'How is it that you know about her current activities if you don't see her?'

Flora Quillin exchanged a glance with her husband.

'She calls – called her mother,' Roland Quillin said. 'Every so often.'

'She gets mail here sometimes,' Flora Quillin offered. 'We forward it over to . . . that place. It's the only address she'd give us.'

Taylor said, 'Did you know she lived there in her van?'

Flora Quillin nodded. 'Can you imagine such a thing? Roland is an accountant, a good decent man, we've been in this parish twenty years now, the people here are some of Roland's best customers –'

Taylor broke in, 'Do you have any idea about any friends or associates of hers we might talk to?'

'Of course not,' Roland Quillin said.

'Enemies?' Kate suggested. As the Quillins shook their heads she asked, 'When was the last time she called here?'

Again the Quillins exchanged glances. 'It was . . . not too recently,' Flora Quillin whispered.

'Could you be more specific?'

'Not recently . . . I don't remember. I'm sorry.'

Kate stared at her. The evasiveness was transparent. But why? What could she possibly be hiding?

Flora Quillin addressed both detectives. 'Do either of you have children?'

'Two boys,' Taylor answered. 'Both of 'em grown and out on their own.'

'Happy Father's Day,' Flora Quillin said.

Taylor's smile was fleeting and uneasy; he flicked a glance at Roland Quillin who did not change expression. Kate looked on in surprise; she had been vaguely aware that Father's Day was imminent but had not realized it was today.

Flora Quillin said to Taylor, 'Maybe you think we're dreadful parents –'

'Not at all, ma'am.'

'How would you feel if you had a daughter and by the time she was fourteen –'

Kate asked, 'Did you try to get her professional help?'

'Of course we did.' Roland Quillin's tone was sharp with bitterness. '*That's* when she came home claiming to be a lesbian. Psychotherapy,' he said scathingly. 'Where else would she get such garbage in her head? *That's* when she found out how easy it was to blame us for everything.'

Kate turned to a new page in her notebook. 'May we have the psychiatrist's name?'

'Why?' Roland Quillin demanded. 'What do you have to talk to her for?'

'We don't know,' Kate said mildly. 'Depending on how this investigation goes, we may not talk to her at all.'

'Marietta Hall,' said Flora Quillin. 'She's in Brentwood.'

Kate recorded the name, and rose. 'We appreciate your courtesy under these circumstances. May we borrow a photo of Dory to use in our inquiries about her?'

'We don't have any,' Flora Quillin said. 'We didn't want one thing of hers in this house.'

Judged and pronounced irredeemable at the age of seventeen. Kate turned away, sickened.

'And her name is Dolores,' Flora Quillin said.

'My apologies,' Kate said. 'I understood she preferred to call herself Dory.'

'Just one more way she strayed from the upbringing of her parents and all the laws of God,' Roland Quillin said.

'Thank you, folks,' Taylor said. 'Good night.'

The detectives got into the car, Taylor behind the wheel. He hunched over it, peering at the barred and darkened house; the lights had been turned off with their departure.

Taylor looked at Kate. 'I'm trying to figure out what one of my boys would have to do for me to toss his ass permanently out on the street. I don't know, Kate — what the hell *do* you do if your kid decides she's gonna be a hooker on Hollywood Boulevard?'

'Ed, I don't know. But can you just write off a child totally, like she was some kind of bad debt? They raised her from a baby . . . now you'd think she was no more than a dead fly.'

Taylor scowled at the house. 'I think the Quillins are possibles.'

Kate looked at Taylor in astonishment.

'Kate, they have a motive — the way Dory fucked up their lives.'

'Be serious, Ed. From what Maggie Schaeffer said, and

the Quillins' own statements, the hatred was purely mutual. Besides, parents don't kill their children.' She added grimly, 'At least not physically.'

'Sometimes you damn well feel like it, Kate,' Taylor said earnestly, 'the things they do. And a second is all it takes to pick up a baseball bat. And you saw the way that dead kid was, the look on her face – like she wanted to hug whoever offed her.'

'If they all hated each other –'

'I don't buy that,' Taylor said. 'Hating your own kid, your own flesh and blood – how can you buy that?'

'But why would they want to do anything to her now? This's been going on since she was fourteen. They threw her out of their lives two years ago, all the damage she did was already done. Why now? What could've happened to make a difference now?'

Taylor shrugged. 'Kate,' he said sadly, 'I know some of them look real young and innocent, but how could anybody be a hooker and look like her?'

'I'm wondering myself,' Kate admitted.

'Christ, she looked like she'd never been touched.'

'Maybe she never felt like she was,' Kate said.

'I've heard . . .' Taylor said, and cleared his throat.

Another of his delicate questions, Kate thought. Part of the game they played, where she knew that Taylor knew she was a lesbian, but neither of them discussed or admitted it – Taylor because he was obviously uncomfortable with the issue, and she because she was convinced that her professional efficiency depended on discretion and silence.

'I've heard that lots of prostitutes are actually lesbians,' he said.

'I've heard that too,' Kate said easily.

'Think it's true?'

'Only if you subscribe to the theory that prostitutes actually hate men.'

'Do all lesbians hate men?'

How the hell should I know, Kate thought in irritation. Am I for chrissakes an expert on all lesbians who ever lived? 'Some do,' she answered. 'Some heterosexual women do, too.'

'But not you, right Kate?' Taylor asked innocuously. 'You think men are okay, don't you?'

'One or two of you,' Kate answered drily.

Taylor chuckled. With a final glance at the darkened Quillin house he pulled away from the curb.

CHAPTER 5

Kate drove unhurriedly down Olympic Boulevard toward the city of Santa Monica, sorting through her thoughts amid the ocean-like flow of late night traffic. Faces filtered through her mind: Maggie Schaeffer; Patton; Roland and Flora Quillin. Andrea Ross. And always Dory Quillin.

After Taylor had gone home Kate had remained at the station to check the Records Unit and verify that indeed Dory Quillin had been arrested as a juvenile, one count of prostitution. Then Kate had reviewed the stack of Field Interview cards compiled by Hansen's officers – interviews with the owners and patrons of the hillside businesses, the staff and guests of the motel. She had learned that fourteen windows of the motel faced onto the parking lot of the Nightwood Bar; guests had occupied nine of those rooms. At approximately six o'clock on a quiet, idyllic Father's Day evening, the killer of Dory Quillin had been lucky; no one was looking out any window facing the parking lot shared by the Casbah Motel and the Nightwood Bar.

If the FI's were this useless in providing leads, Kate reflected dourly, there seemed scant promise in the followup interviews she and Taylor would conduct in the next few days. Unless the technicians found something highly unusual in the Volkswagen van, Dory Quillin would most likely become a statistic among Los Angeles County's criminal violence files, a permanent fixture among the city's uncleared cases. Or perhaps the day would come when some murderous drifter was finally caught here or in some other city, to confess idly, offhandedly, *I knocked off a few other people too. A young girl in L.A. back in '85, with a baseball bat. . . .* And the grisly details of another version of Juan Corona or Henry Lee Lucas would splash across the nation's newspaper headlines. . . .

Kate shrugged impatiently, realizing that she was applying to the Dory Quillin case her own gut theory about uncleared homicides generally – that a significant percentage were committed by anonymous roving monsters, serial killers who drifted from city to city, from state to state, smashing lives without the slightest qualm or remorse for the horrors they perpetrated.

She turned off Olympic and decided that instead of futile pondering of serial killers, she would look forward to the drink she would soon have to end this long day. She pulled into the subterranean garage of her apartment on Montana Avenue wondering why it was that America couldn't produce a decent scotch of its own.

Switching on the lights of her apartment, she frowned at the open window and the newly formed coat of dust on the furniture. Too much wood in here, she'd bought too much wood – a huge teak coffee table, a desk, a bar, cabinets and bookcases, a magazine rack; even the sofa and the lamps were accented in wood – all of it bought more than a year ago.

Needing no tangible symbols of Anne, knowing she would take Anne with her wherever she lived and for as long as she lived, she had sold without regret all the furniture along with their house in Glendale. But she had bought all this wood out of a compulsion to surround herself with substantiality, with objects that suggested solidity and permanence: Anne's death had been too much a taking away of the ground from beneath her.

She splashed scotch generously over ice cubes, cleaning up a few drops on the counter with a bar towel, ruefully aware of her neatness. She had lived with Anne for twelve years in comfortable clutter; now she was obsessed with order.

She checked her answering machine; its light was blinking.

Kate dear, this is Ellen. Can we have lunch this week? Stephie and I are going to the Gay Pride parade this Sunday, then we're off on vacation . . . Can I see you before then?

You're still everybody's favorite cop at Modern Office . . .
mine too. Love you, bye Kate . . .

'Bye, Ellen,' Kate murmured. 'I love you too.'

She took off her jacket and tossed it over a chair, resisting the need to hang it in the bedroom closet. Thinking about Ellen O'Neil and the homicide investigation at Modern Office where she had met Ellen more than a year ago, she went back to the refrigerator to add ice cubes to her drink. She swallowed a quantity of scotch, then selected packaged ham and some cheese for a sandwich. The scotch burned down her throat and became spreading warmth.

What had Andrea Ross said tonight about her lack of response to Dory Quillin's advance? *I needed all of myself for myself.* Five months after Anne's death she herself had needed no less. But that was when she had met Ellen O'Neil – when she had not had an emotional breadcrumb to offer anyone.

She could hardly regret that meeting, or that needful night when Ellen had sheltered her in her arms. *But now I'm coming back to life,* she thought, *some of the dead places are beginning to regenerate. . . .*

Except for the timing of their meeting, Ellen would be waiting for her right now in the quiet dark bedroom down the hall.

Kate took another warming sip of scotch and directed a poisonous thought toward Stephanie Hale. Whatever her opinion of the brittle, self-centred UCLA professor, she had to give her credit: she had fought for Ellen. She had recovered quickly from her astonishment and rage at the threat to a relationship she had deemed safe beyond challenge. She had bought a house to please Ellen, even though the act risked exposure of their relationship to her academic colleagues, even though buying an affordable house meant living in the despised San Fernando Valley. She had even agreed unconditionally to Ellen's career ambitions.

And Ellen had committed herself to making the renewed relationship work. 'I can't even think about you as an alternative,' she had told Kate in her candid way. 'Anne fills up every corner of your life. There isn't room for anyone else.'

There was no ethical choice, as Kate saw it, but to accept

Ellen's decision, to offer Ellen the caring and loyalty of her friendship. Now they had occasional lunches together, a drink after work – whatever time would permit. There was still a tinder-dry attraction between them, and Kate was aware that they were careful with each other, neither of them wanting to do anything to hurt the other.

That night – how long ago had it been? Almost a year and a half since she had wept in the arms of Ellen O'Neil and then afterward, afterward . . . There had been no one else since Ellen, no one remotely tempting or even interesting . . . Until tonight.

She would call Ellen tomorrow, have lunch with her just as soon as she had breathing room in her investigation of the death of Dory Quillin.

Suddenly exhausted, Kate put the food back in the refrigerator and picked up her scotch and walked to her bedroom, her thoughts of Ellen O'Neil fading into the image of Andrea Ross.

CHAPTER 6

Kate parked the Plymouth on Washington Boulevard in front of Wilshire Division's impound garage.

Taylor climbed dispiritedly out of the car and tucked the tail of his yellow sport shirt into his pants, having tossed his jacket and tie onto the back seat. En route he had growled his opinion that this case was a big fat waste of time and would produce a big fat zero for their efforts, and had since lapsed into glumness.

The Volkswagen van was in the last garage of the row along the rear of the lot. 'Baker,' Kate called as she and Taylor entered the metal building, 'we're going in.'

The fingerprint man worked in the front of the van, his bald head very still over the tape he was applying to a latent print on the dashboard. Gray fingerprint powder lay over every exposed surface. He did not reply or lift his head until he had carefully peeled off the transparent tape with its preserved fingerprint. 'Help yourself,' he snapped.

Kate stepped up into the open side door of the van, brushing at particles of fingerprint powder already clinging to her tan jacket and pants. Taylor moved past her, over to the makeshift shelving at the rear of the van, to look down at the bag of dry cat food under the bottom shelf. 'Wonder what happened to the cat,' he said.

Kate was at the white formica table Dory Quillin had used as a desk; it was covered with gray fingerprint powder. She opened its single drawer. Visible were five one hundred dollar bills fanned across the bottom of the drawer, and three clear plastic bags of white powder.

50

'Coke,' Taylor announced from beside her. 'Couple of ounces, wouldn't you say?'

'Looks like it,' Kate said shortly.

'Drugs,' Taylor said. 'So far our angel-faced victim is into women, men, and now drugs. Maybe she was a porno star on the side.'

Kate heard bitterness in the sarcasm; and she realized that he felt the same sense of having been taken in by Dory Quillin that she did.

Taylor pointed to the money. 'The C-notes, payoff money from johns.'

'Probably,' Kate agreed. 'Same with the coke. These days it's the same as money. Ed, if she was making hundred dollar bills and bags of coke, she wasn't getting her clients off the street.'

'Nope.' He rested a hand on the holster at his belt. 'Kate,' he said eagerly, 'if she was turning hundred dollar tricks maybe she had some big shot john she was shaking down.'

Deliberately encouraging his renewed enthusiasm, she offered, 'A very good motive for murder, Ed.' Why not, she thought resignedly. Let's add blackmail to the list.

Taylor nodded. 'The place doesn't look disturbed. If she kept that money and coke here, maybe she's got a list of johns somewhere.'

'Maybe.' She picked up a yellow legal pad which had been lying face down on the table.

'What the hell,' Taylor muttered.

Kate stared at three huge, heavily inked blocks of black print:

S285

S288

S290

Each letter and number was perhaps four inches high by two inches wide; the three blocks filled all but the top of the page. She was reminded of her own habit of drawing outlines of arrows and then filling them in. But none of the absent-minded doodles she made while thinking were ever so large and arresting as these blocks of print which seemed to shout from the page.

Intrigued, puzzled, she decided to book the pad as evidence.

For her own reference she recorded the letters and numbers in her notebook, noticing that each S was decidedly misshapen, with a thickening at its downward curve; she carefully duplicated the shape. She peered at fragments of paper clinging to the top of the pad, the uncapped pen lying next to the pad. 'A page is ripped out,' she said. 'Ed, I think all this could mean something.'

'Yeah,' Taylor said uninterestedly. He bent to one knee to examine paperbacks stacked on the floor along the side of the table.

Distracted from the legal pad, Kate asked with more than professional curiosity, 'What kind of books are they?'

'Novels,' Taylor answered. He picked up one after another. '*Loving Her, Gaywyck, The Lesbian Path* — Jesus, here's one called *Old Dyke Tales*.'

'I get the picture,' Kate said with a grin, thinking that she would like to read any of those books herself. She leaned closer to the yellow legal pad, examining it.

'Baker,' she called, 'could you came back here for a minute and dust something for us?'

With an assenting grunt Baker climbed out of the front of the van.

Kate pointed. 'The top of this page, could you bring the imprint up from the previous page?'

Baker immediately crouched, his eyes level with the table top, and brushed gray dust across the top of the yellow paper. Kate could clearly see: *Sept. 15, 1985*, and below that, at the left hand margin, the letters *De* beginning a word which was cut off by the blocks of writing.

'The fifteenth was Saturday,' Kate said. 'The ripped out page may be around here somewhere.'

'No way,' Baker bristled. 'Her trash bag is between the front seats. Nothing in it but Kleenex.'

'Why would it be here?' challenged Taylor. 'Those letters — ' He gestured to the pad, '— they could be the first two letters of 'Dear.' Maybe she was writing somebody a letter and she mailed it.'

'Very true,' Kate said, pleased with him.

'And how do we know she wrote it Saturday? She could've put that date on it anytime.'

'Also true,' Kate conceded. 'Look, Ed, the pad's new – that ripped out page is the first one. I think she was at this desk making this page of whatever-it-is just before she was killed. See how some of the last number isn't quite filled in? And look at the pen – the cap's off.'

'Kate, lots of people leave caps off pens.'

Kate picked up the pen. 'This one's ink. With a razor point felt tip, which is why the imprint shows on the page beneath. People don't leave caps off felt tip pens.'

'But she was outside the van when she bought it.'

'Somebody came to the van while she was sitting here, she came out –'

'I'll leave you two gumshoes,' Baker said acidly. 'Some of us don't have time to stand around and theorize.'

Kate grinned as he stalked to the door to return to his work. The irascible Baker was an excellent fingerprint technician. 'Ed,' she said, 'maybe you're right about that list of johns, maybe it's here somewhere. Let's take a close look. I'll check out the wicker trunk.'

She unhooked the lid, lifted it. On top, carefully folded, lay a snowy white silk shirt and white silk pants, two pairs of white silk bikini panties, and two matching lace bras, their cup size quite small.

Kate fingered the soft fabric of the shirt. This had to be the clothing Dory Quillin wore to her sexual rendezvous. She had found her ticket off Hollywood Boulevard by understanding – instinctively or otherwise – basic male fantasies. In this white clothing she was young and virginal, she would be many men's fantasies of an angelic young girl – or a young boy.

Other clothing also lay neatly folded in the trunk: conventional panties and bras, socks, shorts, tank tops, jeans, T-shirts, sweatshirts. Clothing the real Dory Quillin wore, Kate thought. These silk garments were a costume, a disguise, a game, a pretence. . . .

She shrugged in exasperation. Again she was romanticizing, again she was constructing a persona from an expression she had perceived in the spectral silver-blue eyes of a dead girl. If anyone should be objective about Dory Quillin, it should be she – the detective in charge of investigating her murder.

From beneath the clothing Kate extracted a white shoulder bag of canvas and plastic weave, streamers hanging from its flap – a teenager's purse. Its contents were neatly arranged, and obviously undisturbed.

Kate used her pen to move objects for a better view. There was a wallet, a long-handled comb, a brush, a compact, a case containing – according to its label – azure eyeshadow, a purse-size package of Kleenex, another pen like the one on the desk, and a small spiral notebook which Kate fished out and opened.

It was not, as she had hoped, an address book. Only the first page of the notebook contained writing:

S285

S288

S290

These had been scrawled, as if in haste or agitation.

Kate pulled out the wallet, a simple folded leather case much like her own, with a pocket for currency, a window showing a driver's license, and several slots for credit cards.

The driver's license showed an unsmiling, off-center photo of Dory Quillin, and a birthdate of 05-03-63; she had been passing herself off as twenty-two. Kate leafed through the currency: a twenty, a five, six ones; the credit card slots held a dozen or so business cards, and a folded sheet of paper.

'Ed,' she said softly.

Taylor turned from inspecting the shelves of Dory Quillin's food provisions. Whistling tunelessly, he examined the business cards Kate spread across the table, and the additional piece of paper she smoothed out; it listed nine names and phone numbers.

'Bingo,' he said. '*Look* at the titles on these business cards, Kate. Execs from General Electric, Wells Fargo, Arco, Bank of America,' he read, 'AT&T, GTE – that's a nice touch, she used both phone companies. Alcoa – that's a nice touch too, maybe they made the bat. Twentieth Century Fox, NBC-TV. And look here, Kate. Smith Barney. Where she made money the old-fashioned way.'

Kate smiled ruefully, then ran a finger down the list of names and numbers on the paper. 'It could be interesting, checking these numbers out.'

'I'm betting they're more listings from the Fortune 500.' Taylor added cheerfully, 'It's a cinch we're gonna have some red-faced captains of industry.'

Kate showed him the notebook. 'Identical to what's on the legal pad. I think this could mean something important, Ed.'

'My bet is, it means shit. Only in novels do victims leave death messages.'

'You could be right,' Kate conceded. 'But I have a feeling . . . There's a lot of work here, Ed. Checking out these new leads, talking again to the women at the Nightwood Bar, Dory's parents. Now that the news has sunk in.'

'A return trip to the Nightwood Bar,' Taylor said. 'This time I wear my bulletproof vest.'

'It might be better if I do it solo,' Kate suggested with a grin. 'I'm not welcome there either, but I fit in a little better than a patriarchal pig.'

'Oink growl,' Taylor said good-naturedly, and returned to the search of Dory Quillin's van.

CHAPTER 7

Walter Phillips was bald, in his fifties, trim and tanned; he wore a black suit subtly pinstriped, a white shirt with a gray tie. As Kate and Taylor made their way across an expanse of oriental carpeting he stood behind his desk, a hand extended; he had instructed his gray-haired secretary to show the detectives right in.

After the ritual of introduction and identification, Kate and Taylor sat down in armchairs in front of a boomerang-shaped teak desk barren except for a sheaf of papers and a computer terminal. Phillips lowered himself into his leather desk chair and looked at the detectives with cordial expectancy.

From a gray City of Los Angeles interoffice envelope Taylor slid a photo of Dory Quillin, a head shot cropped from one of Shapiro's photos. He said politely, 'We have information that you know this person, Mr. Phillips.'

The polished planes of the tanned face froze into immobility as Phillips stared at the glossy of Dory Quillin's face in death. 'What's . . . all this about?' He looked up at Kate; his dark stare pierced her.

'What can you tell us about this person?' Kate repeated coolly, reinforcing Taylor's confrontational approach. To further unsettle him she tapped a finger on the photo Taylor had placed on the desk, to direct his attention back to it.

But he did not look down at the photo; he fixed his stare on Taylor. 'I have a right to know exactly what all this is about.' The voice was firm, authoritative.

Too confident, Kate decided. Well beyond a surprise attack,

their best tactic given this man's probable role in Dory Quillin's life.

Phillips was addressing Taylor in crisp tones: 'I have a right to know exactly what kind of trouble brings the police into my business office under the erroneous supposition that I might be associated with that trouble.'

'You do assume there's trouble,' Kate temporized, watching him, uninterested in the trappings of this spacious corner office high in the Bank of America tower.

Phillips inclined his head toward the photo lying on the expanse of desk, his eyes flicking toward it, then away. 'It doesn't take much imagination to see when that was taken.'

'Yes sir,' Taylor replied. 'And we'd still like you to tell us what you know about her.'

'Not a goddam thing. And certainly nothing at all about her death.'

It was enough; however indirectly, he had admitted knowing Dory Quillin, and Kate pursued him. 'Where did you meet her?'

'I know my rights, Detective. I don't have to answer your questions, I have a right to an attorney.'

'With all respect, sir, we're conducting an inquiry, not making an accusation.'

His eyes met and held Kate's; she matched the strong dark stare with difficulty. But she sensed lessening intensity and then concession in the stare before she heard the words: 'At the Hyatt, in the bar.' He exhaled audibly, then asked, 'What happened?'

'She was killed last night,' Kate answered, still holding his gaze. 'A blow to the head.'

He blinked, looked away from her to the photo, then closed his eyes for a moment. 'Did she . . . suffer?'

At this first sign of humanity in Walter Phillips, Kate felt in herself an involuntary softening. The same question had come from Flora Quillin – but this man had let down a carefully controlled facade to ask it, and the question from him was oddly moving.

'It didn't appear so,' Kate answered gently. 'How did you arrange meetings with her, Mr. Phillips?' She added, 'We're quite aware of her . . . activities.'

He placed his hands on the desk and looked down at them, small hands with tapered fingers, the nails with the buffed gloss of professional manicuring. 'An answering service. She'd call me back.'

'Where did you meet?'

He continued his inspection of his hands. 'At the Hyatt, in the bar. Sometimes she'd wait —' Phillips broke off as if regretting the information he had volunteered, then continued unhappily, '— just around the corner from here.'

'Who told you about her?' Taylor asked.

Phillips' eyes jerked up to him. 'I told you how I met her.'

Kate learned forward. 'Mr. Phillips, major hotels tend to be very careful about unattached women who frequent their bars. We have a list of her male customers, we'll be talking to them all. At this point we're asking only routine questions, it's in your own self-interest to cooperate. Unless you don't mind the problem of more visible —'

'Darryl Smith,' Phillips said. 'Nine floors down.'

Kate remembered the name among those they had developed from Dory Quillin's list of phone numbers.

'Look,' Phillips said, 'she was . . . there were some good times, that's all . . .'

Taylor asked, 'How often did you see her?'

Walter Phillips' gaze drifted to a spot between Kate and Taylor. 'Maybe . . . once a month. Whenever she took a notion to return my calls. Sometimes it might be two weeks or more before she'd call back. She was independent as hell, she was —' Phillips blinked and broke off.

'How much did you pay her?' Taylor inquired.

The dark eyes narrowed, sharpened. 'We had dinner dates. I bought drinks for her, dinner.'

'Your relationship was platonic?' Taylor inquired sarcastically. 'Or are you telling us she was satisfied with drinks and dinner in exchange for her professional services?'

'I have no idea what she did with anyone else and I don't care,' Phillips said, his voice again authoritative. 'We had dinner dates. That's all.'

'Maybe share a little cocaine along with the drinks and dinner, Mr. Phillips?'

'I won't dignify that with an answer.'

Kate listened to this exchange impatiently; Phillips was much too acute to admit the unlawful act of drug possession, much less solicitation of a prostitute. She broke in, 'When did you last see her?'

'More than a month ago. She never did return my last call –' He broke off and his eyes became distant, as if he was examining the finality of those words.

'What kind of person was she?' Kate asked softly, into his reverie.

'She was sweet and funny . . . she laughed at all my jokes. She was unusually pretty, she –' He shrugged. 'What do you expect me to say?'

Something else, she thought. Something better. She asked harshly, 'Where were you Sunday night, Mr. Phillips?'

His stare focused on her again. 'At home,' he said resentfully. He added in a low, grudging tone, 'With my wife. And children. Jesus,' he expelled, 'you won't have to check that out, will you? Jesus Christ –'

'That remains to be seen,' Kate said pitilessly. She closed her notebook, dropped one of her cards onto Phillips' vast desk, and stood. 'We may have further questions,' she said.

Shaking his head, Phillips swiveled in his chair to look out over the towers of the city.

Darryl Smith sent word that he was in a meeting but would be free momentarily; five minutes later he somberly greeted the detectives in the glass-partitioned cubicle which was his office in the auditing department.

A younger, blond version of Phillips but with even less hair, wearing a navy blue suit, Smith sat stiffly upright, glanced expressionlessly at the photo of Dory Quillin, acknowledged aquaintance with her, issued polite but terse answers identical to Walter Phillips', and volunteered nothing further.

At Wells Fargo they received immediate and polite reception and the illusion of cooperation from Thomas Wilson. Also from Robert Stone at AT&T, John Moore at Alcoa, Donald Lee at Arco; and they were given identical answers to each question posed and no substantive detail to provide either fresh information or leads of any kind.

'Christ,' Taylor muttered as he and Kate sat in the

Plymouth completing their notes. 'Everybody on this executive shit list knows we're coming, they're all primed and ready. All these other names to check out, we're gonna end up with worn-out shoe leather, period. Business execs, shit. They're worse than politicians.'

'They passed Dory Quillin from hand to hand like a bag of potato chips,' Kate said bitterly, tiredly, feeling her tiredness like a leaden weight. 'This is a whole new version of the old boy network.'

Taylor tossed his notebook onto the seat between them. 'I bet they'll even alibi whoever's not covered.'

She took a deep breath, expelled it. 'My fault, I should never have told Phillips we had a list. I blew it, Ed.'

'You're kidding, right? The minute we walked out of anybody's office, he'd have been on the horn to his buddies. Too bad we started out with a smart bird like Phillips. But shit, all these birds are smart. It's the dumb crooks we catch, not the smart ones.'

Kate glanced at her watch. 'Let's divide the rest of the names on the list, Ed, and split up. I'll drop you at the station, you might see if anything interesting's come up from the vehicle license numbers at the crime scene. Maybe you could get started on the search warrant we'll need to look at the file on Dory in her psychiatrist's office. Do what you can, then go on home and have a nice dinner at a decent hour with Marie.'

Taylor nodded. 'You go home too, Kate. You look tired. The Nightwood Bar can wait till tomorrow.'

'I want to stay on this. If there's a trail somewhere, I don't want it getting cold.'

Taylor started the Plymouth, then grinned at her. 'Give my regards to Patton.'

Kate smiled at him, thinking instead of Andrea Ross, wondering if she would be at the Nightwood Bar.

CHAPTER 8

After she dropped off Taylor, one more fruitless interview convinced Kate that further contact with the men on Dory Quillin's list could wait; perhaps an interval of a day or two might introduce an element of apprehension and lead to useful inconsistencies in their stories.

Pulling the Plymouth onto the Hollywood Freeway, she admitted that there was no real justification for returning to West Hollywood – only a nagging sense of having unfinished business there. Perhaps a need to see in broad daylight the house and neighborhood where Dory Quillin had grown up and then had run away from when she was only fourteen. Or perhaps to confirm by the light of day two parents who had obliterated from their lives a daughter's existence, unrelenting even in the face of her death.

As she crossed La Brea Avenue into West Hollywood, Kate slowed the Plymouth as much as traffic would allow. With late afternoon yellow sunlight washing the city, she cruised along Santa Monica Boulevard, happy to be without Taylor beside her, happy to look at the clothing shops and restaurants and sidewalk cafes and all the street activity, euphoric as a child on a summer vacation. She knew that the source of her pleasure was sheer geographic location: the symbolism of this city, a city where she was welcome, a place where she belonged.

Roland Quillin was in his yard kneeling in the flowerbed lining the edge of the house, working a short-handled hoe at

61

the base of a rosebush, turning the soil into soft loam. Watching his diligence, Kate walked across the lawn.

As if he felt the vibration of her footsteps, his rhythmic hoeing slowed; he looked around at her and soberly nodded. With a tense, resentful squaring of his shoulders he resumed his labor.

'Sorry to disturb you,' she said to his back, not minding the discourtesy. 'Is Mrs. Quillin at home?'

He squatted on his heels, earthen stains on the knees of his gray cotton pants, and wiped a shirt-sleeve across his forehead; the curved scar on his cheekbone looked pinkish white in the sun. 'She's resting, she had cancer surgery a few months ago. She's tired today, I'd just as soon not disturb her.'

'Of course,' Kate said with immediate sympathy, reminded again that many people's lives contained no less grief than her own. 'I hope she's recovering without too many problems.'

'Well, it was cervical, they think they got it all. She saw the doctor again this morning, it always takes a lot out of her.' He knelt again and continued his hoeing. 'No offense, I hope the police won't have to bother us anymore. We don't know anything about what's happened to Dolores. She's alone with God now, enduring His judgment.'

Broodingly, Kate watched Roland Quillin scoop and shape dirt around the rosebushes, dark hair matted along his thick arms, dirt-stained gloves protecting his hands. Obviously, neither a night's sleep nor this reproachfully bright new June day had brought any fresh perspective to the Quillins.

'I have only a few questions,' she finally said. 'Do you know the name of the black woman your daughter brought here and how we might reach her?'

The hoeing did not stop. 'No idea whatsoever, me nor Flora either. Dolores must have told us but we put it right out of our minds.'

'Do you have any idea why your daughter would take a trip up into Central California a few days before she was killed?'

The hoe stilled, then resumed its activity, stabbing at the soil. 'No idea at all,' Roland Quillin said.

There's something here, Kate decided. With deliberate slowness she pulled her notebook out of her shoulder bag.

Roland Quillin stopped hoeing and again sat back on his haunches as she made a note of her exact question and his reply.

He stood, removed his gardening gloves, stuffed them into a back pocket. 'If you have more questions, let's go inside,' he said curtly. 'This isn't any of the neighbors' business.'

'I have no more questions right now,' Kate said. 'I hope Mrs. Quillin feels better soon.' She added evenly, 'I'll be back in touch.'

Kate parked on La Brea. The street was quiet, shadowy, its businesses shuttered for the night. She walked up the dimly lit hill toward the Nightwood Bar, noticing that at ten o'clock the drapes on all the windows in the Casbah Motel were drawn; either the guests were early risers, or, more likely, there were few guests.

By contrast the interior of the Nightwood Bar seemed exceedingly bright. From the entryway she glimpsed Andrea Ross sitting alone at a small table reading a magazine. Kate pulled her attention quickly away to assess the room, nodding to Maggie Schaeffer who leaned against the cash register, arms crossed, gazing at Kate; she was clad in beige pants and a long-sleeved lavender shirt with a pale lavender armband.

There were perhaps fifteen women present, seemingly a good crowd for a Monday night, but the place felt oddly quiet. On the bar television set, its volume set so low that she could hear only a low buzz of dialogue, Chris Cagney argued vehemently with a stolid Mary Beth Lacey. From the pool table there was a click and clash of balls; a woman in faded jeans with frayed back pockets briefly inspected her handiwork then leaned over to sight her next shot, her sweat-suit-clad opponent looking on, pool cue held on her shoulder like a rifle.

At the bar, their backs to her, Patton sat with Roz; next to Patton were the two black women Kate had interviewed yesterday, Raney and Audie. At a table, Kendall sat between Ash and Tora, all three with chins in hand, their gazes focused on a Scrabble board. All the women in the bar wore identical armbands; Kate noticed a basket of lavender bands on the end of the bar next to the glass bowl filled with coins to benefit the fight against AIDS.

Patton swiveled on her stool. Staring at Kate she pushed back her yacht cap, then nudged Roz, said something to Raney. One by one the women at the bar turned to look at Kate.

In no hurry to advance into the quiet room, Kate moved over to the jukebox and saw that it was dark – one reason for the abnormal silence, and another symbol of the respect accorded to Dory Quillin by Maggie Schaeffer and the women in the bar. Kate glanced at a few of the music selections: 'You Needed Me,' 'Just One Look,' 'Don't Go Breaking My Heart,' 'More Than A Woman' – Anne Murray, Linda Ronstadt, Elton John, the Bee Gees . . . Old stuff, middle of the road pop rock, the kind she had grown to love because it was Anne's music. . . . She gripped the sides of the jukebox, angry that these unexpected, pitiless strikes of memory were still so debilitating, that she still could not deal with this kind of pain.

Straightening her shoulders, she walked purposefully to the bar.

Patton was still staring at her, her light blue eyes cool and mocking. 'So,' she said around the cigarette dangling from a corner of her mouth, 'how's the murder business?'

Apparently Patton's perspective, like the Quillins', had not changed overnight. Kate replied expressionlessly, 'We never have a slow day.'

Raney chuckled, a low sound. The cigaretteless corner of Patton's mouth turned up; she continued to stare at Kate.

'It's nice to see you again,' Maggie Schaeffer said in firm tones to Kate. 'Can the house buy you a drink?'

'No, but thanks.' Kate smiled, appreciating her warmth. 'One of these days I'll come in here off-duty.'

Patton snorted.

'I hope so,' Maggie responded. 'You'll be very welcome.'

Kate raised her voice only slightly to be heard throughout the quiet bar. 'I have information that Dory Quillin had a lover who was with her for a while.' She stood with her body placed carefully, her back toward Andrea Ross, to be certain that inadvertent eye contact would not reveal Andrea as the source of this information.

Kate continued, 'The woman is black –'

'That really narrows it down,' Raney said.

The room erupted in laughter. Grinning at Raney, Kate finished, '– and her first name is Neely.'

Silence returned to the bar; even the click of the pool balls had ceased. Kate waited with very little hope. Undoubtedly there had been considerable conversation among all these women, and if they were not hostile toward this investigation, surely they were fearful. The homicide of a lesbian who was linked with drugs and prostitution was a morass few people would willingly entangle themselves in, much less woman with their own individual anxieties about exposure.

'We need to talk to her,' Kate explained. 'We need to learn more about the victim –'

'Victim,' Patton repeated bitterly. 'Why don't you call Dory by a number?'

'Patton, stuff it up your knapsack,' Maggie growled. She said to Kate, 'You might check out the other bars around town. Peanuts, the Palms –'

'Not Peanuts,' Audie said, 'it's a place for teeny boppers, it's –' Meeting Patton's glare, she choked off into silence.

Definitely Peanuts, Kate decided. If Dory Quillin was any indication, the woman named Neely had a taste for very young women. 'Thanks,' she said to Maggie. She raised her voice. 'Does anyone know Neely's last name?'

Again there was silence.

Tired and disappointed, conceding defeat, Kate sought the eye of Andrea Ross to nod goodnight. But Andrea gestured to her.

Feeling the eyes of the entire bar on her, Kate walked to Andrea's table and said in a low tone, 'I don't want to give you a problem here.'

Andrea smiled. 'Sit down, Typhoid Mary.'

Kate pulled out a chair. 'However this case turns out, I'll be glad when it's over,' she muttered. Then she looked at Andrea in pleasure.

Her dark hair, pulled into an artfully twisted pile behind her head, conveyed the same effect as the tight-fitting cap she had worn last night: it unobtrusively framed her regal face. She wore an oversize shirt a vivid shade of coral, its shapelessness tantalizing with its suggestion of the ripeness of her body. Kate looked down at Andrea's fingers, which were tracing the rim of her glass, thinking that never in her life had a woman made so instantaneous and stirring a physical impact on her, not even Anne.

She cleared her throat. 'These two bars that Maggie mentioned, are they near here?'

Andrea nodded. 'I can do even better. Neely could be at one of them tonight – and since I know what she looks like, I thought you might like me to come with you.'

'I'd be grateful,' Kate said quietly, feeling the heavy pulse beat in her throat.

Maggie approached the table with a tray. 'You can always use some coffee,' she said gruffly, serving Kate and placing a cocktail napkin next to, not under, the coffee mug.

'Maggie, I really appreciate it,' Kate said. She picked up her mug and sipped from it, palming the napkin with her other hand. She glanced at the napkin, slid it into her jacket picket. On the underside was written MALONE.

Andrea looked at her with bright eyes, obviously having missed nothing. She smiled. 'Ready to go, Detective Delafield?'

During this second trip of the day into West Hollywood Kate was distracted from the landscape by the presence of the woman beside her, by the sensual fragrance of musk filling her nostrils.

'I haven't been here in such a long time,' Andrea said softly, looking around her with interest. 'Except for going to the Nightwood Bar, I don't get out of my own territory much.'

'Nor me,' Kate replied. Hoping to elicit more personal information from Andrea she offered, 'It seems I divide all my time between home in Santa Monica and working at Wilshire Division.'

'It's the Silverlake district and Echo Park for me,' Andrea responded.

Kate searched for other conversation, innocuous topics that would not be construed as a ferreting out of information by an LAPD detective. She had not felt this awkward since her early teens. 'The music on the jukebox back there,' she said, 'I haven't heard some of those songs in years.'

'Neither had I,' Andrea said, her low voice distant, melancholy. 'Is there anything that can hurt more than music? Just the line of a song – and a whole period of your life comes flooding back . . . All those memories, all that emotion . . .'

'I couldn't agree more,' Kate said.

In the unbroken silence that followed, Kate understood that she had chosen the one topic guaranteed to fully shut off communication. She shared a common anguish with this woman, but neither of them wished to reveal her pain, much less explain it.

She made a U-turn around the median strip on Santa Monica Boulevard and found a parking space in front of the neon-lit massage parlor next to the Palms. The bar looked ordinary enough; then Kate opened her car door to rock music pouring from the doorway a good fifty feet away. As she approached the bar the beat seemed to bounce up from the pavement. She thought: I'm going to *hate* this place. . . .

The entryway was festooned with signs, among them a boldly lettered warning that two pieces of ID were required including one with a photo. Deafened by the blasting music, Kate followed Andrea into a long narrow room dim and cool, acrid with the smell of beer and smoke.

A dozen or so patrons, as many men as women, were scattered along the bar or at tables against the wall. There were two bartenders; Kate felt their eyes on her as she followed Andrea through this room and into another in the back which reverberated with sound, its dance floor lit with stage lights, the walls lined with neon that flashed to the thundering beat as a male singer shrieked, *I love rock 'n roll music!* At the side of the room a disc jockey sat in a glass-enclosed cage gazing out with glassy-eyed boredom. Two couples were at tables, one of the couples male. On the dance floor two young women spun, twisted, bobbed and dipped in unison. Kate's ears buzzed; she could feel vibration in the floor, moving up her legs and through her body.

Andrea shook her head, turned and headed back toward the outer room. Pausing at the doorway, a hand on Kate's arm, her lips close to Kate's ear to be heard, she said, 'Why don't you write a note, leave it with the bartender?'

Kate took out one of her cards. Leaning on a shelf which was designed to hold drinks beside several high-backed stools, she wrote: TO NEELY MALONE. CALL ME. I'M TRYING TO HELP.

As she capped her pen, Andrea picked up the card.

'I'll take care of it,' Kate shouted over the din.

Again Andrea's lips were close to her ear: 'It's best to let me. You act too much like a cop.'

Andrea sauntered over to the bar, to the service area. When one of the bartenders came over Andrea beckoned her closer and spoke to her, sliding the card into the bartender's shirt pocket, Kate could see a bill wrapped around the card. Then, without looking at Kate, Andrea walked to the entrance; Kate followed.

She opened the car door for Andrea. 'Thanks. How much do I owe you?'

'Five. I thought she'd be more inclined to watch out for Neely. Why don't you make out another card for Peanuts? If Neely's not there I'll do my same act. You can wait in the car.'

Extracting two five dollar bills from her wallet, Kate smiled and shook her head, still recovering from the shock waves of the music. 'Have times really changed this much? I've never felt so damn old in all my life.'

Andrea chuckled. 'You should be here on weekends. A cover charge, two-drink minimum – and it's packed to the rafters with lesbians who look like they're fourteen years old.'

Again Kate shook her head.

She drove back to the Nightwood Bar talking easily in answer to Andrea's questions about her background – about growing up in Michigan, her parents, her stint in military service and the stretch in Vietnam, her career at LAPD.

In the parking lot of the Nightwood Bar, as Andrea opened her car door, Kate boldly turned to her to ask if she might call; but Andrea reached to her, silencing her with cool soft fingers that seemed to burn the side of Kate's neck with their gentleness.

'I'll be seeing you soon,' Andrea said. And she was gone.

CHAPTER 9

The autopsy was like any other except that Kate focused on the pathologist's hands and did not look at Dory Quillin's face, not even when Mitchell's saw opened her cranium. Fixedly she watched the full length incision in the torso which other homicide detectives ghoulishly referred to as 'canoeing the body.' As always, the chemical smell of the place was corrosive in her nostrils; she felt it invading her clothes, seeping into her pores.

In the chill room which was quiet except for the pathologist's drone into his microphone, she observed attentively, asking no questions as the internal organs of Dory Quillin were measured and weighed and evaluated, and the technical terminology for the trauma to the left side of her brain was uttered into the microphone as the official cause of death.

Taylor asked only one question, and in one word: 'Drugs?'

'No needle tracks,' Mitchell answered mechanically, intent on his work. 'Only slight traces of cocaine in the urine samples. Tissue samples may say differently but right now there's no other indication.'

Kate and Taylor walked out of USC Medical Center.

Taylor grunted with the effort of loosening his tie. 'So now we know. She died from having her head bashed in.'

'Meet you at eleven,' she said curtly, in no mood for his sarcasm. He knew as well as she did that an autopsy could reveal new information and bring new leads in a homicide investigation.

Completing a yawn, Taylor nodded. He never alluded to

Kate's custom of going home immediately after an autopsy unless compelling reasons prevented her.

He said disgustedly, 'We gotta waste time checking out the rest of Dory's useless john list. We gotta waste more time with Dory's shrink trying to figure out what was in this kid's fucked-up head. Shit, Kate.'

Kate squinted at him in bright sunlight unusual for a June morning in Southern California. Her jacket felt warm, increasingly uncomfortable. 'Finding out what was in her head might give us a way to go, Ed. Marietta Hall seems like our next logical bet.' And probably our last hope, she thought dispiritedly.

Kate swung onto the Santa Monica Freeway. Twenty minutes later she was in her apartment stripping off every piece of clothing as if it were contaminated, sealing it all inside a plastic bag to be laundered and dry cleaned. She took a paper sack of pepper from the bathroom cabinet, put her face down into it, and inhaled. Sneezing convulsively, tears streaming, she stepped under scalding shower spray. Twenty minutes later, her sanitized body dressed in fresh clothing, she was on her way to San Vicente Boulevard in Brentwood, the windows of the Plymouth open to complete the drying of her hair, the smell and feel – if not the memory – of the autopsy room gone.

'Christ,' Taylor muttered, his voice so low that only Kate could hear.

Dr. Marietta Hall's office was a thicket of huge plants – ficus, corn plants, schefflera – a dozen or more of them in low, barrel-sized green pots. Vast hot-colored prints of gigantic orange flowers and red and green birds hung on the bright yellow walls. The doctor's slab desk was made of ash so lightly finished that the wood looked raw, as did the matching bookcase which overflowed with looseleaf binders and fat textbooks. The desk was surrounded by four thickly cushioned black velvet modular chairs shaped like the inside of a spoon.

Kate looked around for the traditional psychiatrist's couch and could not locate one amid the shrubbery, unless a hammock qualified; it was strung between four floor-to-ceiling poles painted with black enamel and positioned in front of the picture window overlooking San Vicente Boulevard.

Marietta Hall's hair hung in two gray frizzy wedges just above her shoulders. Her face, heavily tanned, was etched by two deep wrinkles like parentheses around a wide, thin, sharp-edged mouth. A fine network of crow's feet lay at the corners of lake-blue eyes that were guileless in their glancing survey of Taylor, penetrating in their assessment of Kate.

She stood to shake hands, a towering woman in white pants and an embroidered denim shirt, her body thin through the arms and chest, thickening out through the stomach and hips. The hand Kate grasped was big, rough-textured and warm, like a farmer's hand, the grip iron-firm. Kate liked her.

Producing her identification, introducing herself and Taylor, Kate felt somewhat overmatched by the imposing, bristling presence of Marietta Hall in this startling office. 'We appreciate you taking the time to see us,' she began.

'Not at all. This is normally lunch time for me.' The doctor's tones and enunciation were throaty, Garboesque. 'And I'm making another of my useless attempts to diet.'

Hurriedly Kate reached into her shoulder bag for the search warrant. Polite small talk was one thing, but she drew the line at the deadly boredom of diets. She handed the warrant across the desk. 'Dr Hall, we're investigating the death of a former patient of yours. Dolores Marie Quillin. She was killed Sunday night.'

'Oh Goddess.' Marietta Hall dropped the warrant onto her desk, sat down abruptly in her desk chair, ran a hand across her face and then into the gray hair, stirring it into unruliness.

'Oh Goddess what a tragedy.' The sonorous voice seemed to weight the words with magisterial gravity. She gestured to the detectives. 'Do sit down.' She rubbed her face again, the fingertips kneading around her eyes. 'And do give me a moment.'

Taylor looked uncertainly at the unusual chairs, raised his eyebrows to Kate, then folded his bulk into one, a look of pleasure spreading across his face. Kate settled herself into the chair beside him; it felt sinfully comfortable. She took out her notebook.

Marietta Hall pressed her intercom. 'Jack dear,' she said, 'bring me the file on Dory Quillin. It's under Q.' She flipped off the switch and said to the detectives, 'If I don't tell him he'll look under K and tell me he can't find it. The Californian school system, what are they teaching children these days? It surely can't be spelling.'

Kate shook her head. 'Our own police academy had to put in remedial classes.'

A thin young man in light cotton pants and a yellow tunic came in with a folder. Marietta Hall took the folder and slid in the warrant, then handed it back. 'Make a copy of everything in here right away, will you dear? The original file will be leaving the office.' She dismissed him with a fond smile and a nod.

'A tragedy,' she repeated. 'An utter waste that only the Goddess can explain. I must tell you I'm shocked but not surprised. But I hoped, dammit I *hoped* . . . I thought she might be one of the ones who could . . . What happened, as if I couldn't guess?'

'What's your guess?' Kate asked before Taylor could answer.

'Some psychopath . . . I could never make Dory believe that any man she met might be a killer. She'd just grin at me, she thought she could handle anything. . . .' Grimacing, she stared down at the hands clasped on her desk top. 'Is that what happened?'

'It may turn out to be so,' Kate said gently. 'But the circumstances of her death make it questionable.' Briefly, she described the scene at the Nightwood Bar. 'We understand from Mr. and Mrs. Quillin that you treated Dory after she first ran away from home.'

'Before that. I first saw her when she was twelve.'

Kate exchanged a startled glance with Taylor.

Marietta Hall ran a blunt fingernail over a pattern in the grain of her ash desk. 'The school sent her. She'd made an accusation of sexual molestation against a male gym teacher.'

'Dr. Hall, please elaborate for us,' Kate said tensely, all of her senses alert.

'It was around this time seven years ago, I remember it clearly as yesterday. School was about to let out for summer vacation. I was nearly dead from overwork, but oh Goddess, all those neglected and battered and abused children . . . In those days I was associated with L.A. County social service as well as the school system, you see. I still do occasional consulting work for the County but. . . .'

Burnout, Kate thought sympathetically. Not much wonder she went into private practice. Who could bear for very long all those children with their broken minds and bodies?

The doctor spread her large tanned hands on the desk and examined them. 'Dory claimed the young man had forcibly put his hands down inside her panties, then attempted penile penetration. She was given a pelvic examination of course — there was no physical evidence of any kind. And when it came right down to specifics — to actual times and circumstances — her whole story fell apart.'

She looked up at Kate. 'I'm convinced Dory knew very well that it would. It was her way of trying to draw attention to what was really happening.' The doctor paused.

'Which was?' Taylor prompted.

'Obviously this will take more than a few minutes.' The doctor pressed the intercom. 'Jack dear, bring in the coffee pot and two extra mugs, will you?' She lapsed into silence, staring at Kate.

Disconcerted by the gaze, annoyed by the possibility that this psychologist was indulging in theatrics, Kate capped her Flair pen and looked down at her notes until the tunic-clad young man had left the room.

The doctor poured coffee into two mugs and handed them to Kate and Taylor, then filled a blue mug bearing a figure plucking out daisy petals which read I'M SANE alternating with other petals stating I'M INSANE. Kate took several appreciative sips, thinking that she was drinking far too much coffee lately. Placing her mug on a corner of the ash desk, she uncapped her pen.

'I have no proof,' Marietta Hall said in her low resonant tones, 'but I'm convinced Dory Quillin couldn't stand facing another summer away from school. Because she would be constantly accessible and constantly molested. By her father.'

Kate's pen froze over her notebook, then recorded Marietta Hall's exact statement.

'Her father.' Taylor's voice was flat, skeptical. 'You *suspect* this right? She never actually *told* you, correct?'

'Of course you're correct,' Marietta Hall said with some asperity. 'You know very well I'd have been required by law to make a police report. I would only rejoice at seeing any child abuser arrested and branded as such.'

'Since she'd lied about this gym teacher,' Kate said evenly, 'why did you infer sexual abuse at all?'

'Anyone who works with troubled youngsters automatically looks for it,' Marietta Hall told her, the sharp edge still in her tone, her blue eyes cold. 'We have statistics that tell us to look. One out of every four female children in this country is a victim of sex abuse. And ninety percent of that abuse occurs right in the home.'

She crossed her arms, resting her elbows on the ash desk, and leaned toward Kate. 'In Dory's case the pattern was all too familiar, the evidence was classic. She was withdrawn from her peer group – had no friends at all. She was the brightest kind of youngster, yet totally lacking in self-esteem. Fearful, mistrustful of authority figures, myself included. By the time I first saw her she'd burned herself I don't know how many times, cut herself, fallen and broken bones – you name it. Her parents thought she was accident-prone, but it was the classic self-destructive behavior of a molested child. She slept badly, had frequent nightmares. There were whole periods in her life she'd blanked out. And she was obsessed with all things sexual, she'd ask sexual questions or make sexual references and jokes without any reason at all.'

Marietta Hall ran a disheveling hand through her hair, sighed, took a deep swallow of coffee. 'All that was left to complete the pattern was running away, and less than two years later she did just that, and her parents sent her back to me.'

'Why are you so positive it was the father?' Taylor crossed an ankle over a knee and propped up his notebook. 'Why not an uncle, a neighbor?'

'Because Dory had turned against him. That's also part of the pattern, you see. Children *always* love their parents –

they're *stuck* with loving them until they have the most compelling reasons to stop. Some children never understand even into adulthood that they have every right to withdraw their love from a parent, they live with the fairytale belief that loving a despicable parent will some day change that parent.'

Kate asked quietly, 'Dr. Hall, why wouldn't she admit to you what was happening to her?'

After a swift glance at Taylor the doctor said slowly, carefully, 'Am I correct that you've . . . not known or at least not had an in-depth conversation with a victim of sex abuse?'

'I've worked Juvenile,' Kate temporized, realizing that the doctor was giving her a chance to protect herself should she not want to answer so delicate a question in front of Taylor. 'But police officers, whatever our sensitivity, don't and simply can't have the same relationship with a victim as professionals like yourself.'

'Of course not,' Marietta Hall said, watching her. 'And many professionals enter the field because they're determined not to have other victims suffer as much or as long as they did.'

Kate felt impaled by the gaze. She admitted, 'Someone close to me . . . was molested when she was small.' She shifted with her discomfort, remembering the night Anne had told her of the uncle who had taken her down into a basement and felt her genitals while bringing her hand to his penis and having seven-year-old Anne masturbate him. All those years later Anne had lain in Kate's arms shaking with the renewed ugliness of memory, the renewed sense of shame and violation. . . .

The doctor nodded. 'Often a child never reveals what's happened because she's too ashamed, often she even feels somehow responsible. Sometimes the child has been warned into silence.'

Marietta Hall fixed her stare on Taylor and wagged a finger at him. 'And if it's a parent telling you that you must not reveal what he's doing, you believe him absolutely – after all, he's your father, he's the strongest authority figure in your life.'

Taylor abruptly removed his ankle from his knee and sat

up straight in the spoon-like chair as the doctor continued, 'In Dory's case I do know this: she was well aware of what commonly happens when a child does come forward – the family unit is smashed. The conflicts suffered by abused children are ghastly beyond all imagination, and Dory was in such agony that she had to tell someone, you see, but rather than accuse her father she blamed a perfectly innocent young man, hoping that all the attention drawn to her would make the abuse stop.'

Taylor cleared his throat. 'You said there was no actual sign . . . no physical evidence –'

'Detective Taylor, many abusers use sexual practices other than intercourse.' An agitating hand stirring her frizzy hair into ever wilder disarray, she leaned across the desk toward Taylor. 'A lot of men use that as justification – it's not intercourse so it really doesn't count, there's nothing wrong with putting your penis between your daughter's legs without penetrating her, there's nothing wrong with putting your penis into her mouth –'

'I don't have a daughter,' Taylor uttered from deep in his chair, 'only sons.'

'Of course,' Marietta Hall said in her usual throaty voice, leaning back. 'Forgive the choice of words. I was speaking generally.' She said in an even softer voice, 'Boys also come in for their own share of abuse, you know.'

Letting Taylor reassemble his composure, Kate asked, 'Did you convey your suspicions to Flora Quillin?'

Marietta Hall sighed, opened the top drawer of her desk and took out a long thin cigarette wrapped in dark brown paper, and lighted it. An aroma containing a hint of pipe tobacco reached Kate.

'Not that first time. Without an admission of some kind from Dory, I had to be extremely careful about anything I said to her mother. Once the matter of the gym teacher was cleared up, I did convey my suspicion that some kind of abuse had indeed occurred. But Mrs. Quillin was convinced that Dory had concocted the whole episode out of a fevered pre-adolescent imagination.'

From a desk drawer Marietta Hall took out a plastic replica of a human brain, flipped open a hinged flap in the top, and

76

tapped in cigarette ash. 'I did hope along with Dory that the attention drawn to her would warn her father off, would cause the molestation to stop. It does stop at some point, you see. When the child reaches a certain maturity, or when the perpetrator finally sees a threat to himself. And I told Dory she had to have help, she –'

Kate interrupted, 'Before this incident with the gym teacher, do you think Dory ever tried to tell her mother?'

'If she ran the risk, she lost.' Marietta Hall reached into the brain and stubbed out her cigarette, examined the long butt, tossed it back inside. 'There is no greater risk for a child than to tell the mother. It is the *ultimate* risk. Where else can the child go to find love? If the mother rejects the truth when the child does come forward, that child has nowhere left to turn – she's literally lost both parents. And I can tell you this: a very common response from many mothers is denial. And I mean *complete* denial. Denial at any cost. Denial of evidence right in front of their eyes. Because that mother cannot face the ultimate meaning of what that child has told her. Many women see no escape from their domestic situations, and so they turn against their own child because they can't bear the sight of their own jail cell. Other mothers do something even more despicable – they trick the child into self-blame, accuse her of enticement, make her believe she's responsible.'

'Dr. Hall,' Kate asked quietly, 'you never got so much as an oblique admission out of Dory that this was going on?'

Kate was startled by Marietta Hall's smile, its brilliance. Then she saw that the doctor's clear blue gaze was focused beyond her, on her own memories.

'Dory had the most wonderful quicksilver mind. She never trusted me, she wouldn't trust any adult figure, but she liked me. My sessions with her – it was like pursuing a clever, enchanting little sprite through a maze. I loved being with that beautiful blonde child, she was so bright and . . . well, there are children you work with that you just treasure . . . And she seemed even that much more precious because of what was going on . . .'

Taylor said, 'She came back here two years later. Did she say anything at all to you then?'

'No, not even then. She came back only because her parents didn't know what else to do with her, and she'd been willing to see me before. She was much less frightened but no less evasive.'

Kate said, 'Her parents indicated to us that by then she was involved with prostitution.'

'Yes. They were so much more astounded by that than I was. She'd fallen in with an older prostitute working out of a Hollywood massage parlor, she'd found the one quick way to make money, to break away from her family whenever she wanted to.' The doctor added wryly, 'Dory perceived it as independence.'

Taylor asked, 'Was this prostitute a lesbian?'

Marietta Hall looked at him. 'How on earth should I know?'

Taylor said, 'You're not aware Dory was a lesbian?'

'Of course. You consider that a major news item?'

Taylor said sarcastically, 'I think it's a little weird that she wouldn't confirm all your theorizing about her father but she told you she was a lesbian. When did this come out,' he demanded, 'the first time you saw her or the second?'

'The second.' Glaring at Taylor, Marietta Hall pulled a hairbrush from a desk drawer and yanked it through her hair; the frizzy strands crackled as they were forced back into the wedges framing the doctor's face. She said, 'It helped immeasurably to explain the depth of her trauma. All molested children are damaged, but one can only imagine the suffering of a lesbian child at the hands of a male child abuser.'

'Tell me something.' Taylor's tone had changed, from harshness to curiosity. 'Do you think the molestation – if it happened – might have turned her into a lesbian?'

'To repeat myself, one out of four women in this country has been sexually abused. Are one-fourth lesbian?'

Maybe, Kate thought, half-amused at the exchange.

The doctor shrugged impatiently. 'How can anyone know that? If you'd been molested as a little boy, would that have turned you gay?'

Taylor growled, 'Any bastard who ever tried that –'

'Please, spare me all the macho things you'd have done.'

Marietta Hall turned to Kate. 'The second time Dory was here she told me she had sexual feeling for women, and only for women. And she'd felt that way all her life. She had not, by the way, acted as yet on these feelings.'

Kate asked out of her own curiosity, 'How did you handle that? What did you say to her?'

'I told her it was okay to have those feelings. It may be,' the doctor said reflectively, 'the first time anyone ever told her a feeling of hers was okay. I warned her not to drop this news on her parents, but of course I should have guessed that with so self-destructive a personality, it would be the first thing she'd do. And that was the last time I saw her. I did, however, hear from the parents.'

The doctor smiled sardonically. 'The mother called. Said I should be boiled in oil. Accused me of putting sinful garbage in her daughter's head, threatened to sue. Maybe Dory laid it all on her at once — that she was a lesbian and her father a child molester. Who knows?'

'The male gym teacher,' Kate said, 'he's still in the L.A. school system?'

'No.' She looked stricken. 'Oh Goddess, that was — Dory had no way of knowing what she caused with her accusation . . . The young man envisioned prison bars, I suppose — who wouldn't? He furnished the names of his lovers — there were only two. Both of them men.'

'Jesus,' Taylor expelled. 'Half the world —' He broke off.

Marietta Hall flicked a cold glance over him. 'He was a secondary school teacher, just enough people were privy to what he'd admitted . . . A quiet administrative transfer was arranged.'

Kate said, 'We'll need his name and where to contact him.'

With a sigh, Marietta Hall slid back the cover on a large rolodex and leafed through it. 'This information is seven years old, of course. Carl was such a fine young man —'

'Maybe not so fine,' Taylor said. 'Maybe he got even with this kid for messing up his life.'

'Detective Taylor, most people heal their wounds and go on. Few of us go around avenging the pain of our lives. Most of us will settle for simple acknowledgment of our pain.'

'We still need to talk to him.'

'Of course you do,' Marietta Hall said, writing on a scratch pad. 'May I trust that you won't surround his home with a SWAT team?' She tore off the sheet and handed it to Kate.

Smiling, glancing at the paper, Kate said, 'I guarantee maximum discretion.' The name was Carl Brickwell, at an address in Modesto, California. Dory Quillin had taken a trip to Central California. . . .

From her shoulder bag Kate took a photocopy of the writing she had found in Dory Quillin's van, and unfolded it. 'Dr. Hall, does this mean anything at all to you?'

The doctor spread the sheet of paper on the desk and peered down at it, massaging under her eyes as she concentrated. Again the numbers stared tantalizingly at Kate:

S285
S288
S290

'It seems like it should,' the doctor finally said. 'It truly does. Those numbers bring a vibration, it's in me somewhere what they are.'

'Take your time,' Kate encouraged.

The doctor ran a fingertip over an S. 'This odd shape on each of the letters is intentional, it means something. . . .'

Finally she shook her head. 'Could I keep this copy, think about it?'

'Of course.' Kate rose, took out one of her cards. Taylor struggled out of his chair and onto his feet.

'Jack will have Dory's file ready for you to take. And I'll call you if I figure out these numbers. And you will stay in touch with me,' Marietta Hall said, her tone a sonorous order. 'I do care very much, you see. I've never forgotten that young girl and I never will.'

CHAPTER 10

Kate slowed the Plymouth, peering up at the Casbah Motel
and its adjacent Turkish restaurant. With Taylor dozing
beside her, she drove around the block.

Orange Drive, the street behind the Nightwood Bar, was
lined with old two-story stucco homes sun-faded into muted
colors, the roofs of dusty red tile. All the lawns were small
and neat and made bright by occasional clusters of asters,
zinnias, pansies, nasturtium. Typical of many Los Angeles
streets, there were few trees — only two or three of any size.
One handsome building stood out, gray with blue awnings,
cool-looking with its large shade tree and well-tended
shrubbery. Kate turned at the corner and cruised the short
block to La Brea, admiring the startling beauty of scarlet
hibiscus virtually covering the roof of a white frame house.

S285, S288, S290. The cryptic figures taunted her. They
were somehow connected with Dory Quillin's death — of that
she was certain.

She circled the block once more. On Orange Drive an
older black man had come out to tend his tiny lawn. The
neighborhood, Kate knew, had been fully integrated for well
over a decade. She gazed up behind the stucco houses at the
heavily wooded hill that separated this neighborhood from
the Nightwood Bar. There seemed no logical reason why a
killer or killers would attempt access to the crime scene over
this hill and then over a high redwood fence, but still the
street had been canvassed by Hansen's officers. No one on
the block had noticed anything unusual this past Sunday
evening, Father's Day. . . .

Thinking balefully about Roland Quillin, she turned the car toward the station. She and Taylor would spend the balance of this day on other pending cases, on the most pressing aspects of followup and paperwork; then she would return here tonight. The discoveries of this day notwithstanding, she had to develop more information about Dory Quillin's current life, not her past. She had to find Neely Malone. Tonight she would question individual women until she gleaned something she could use.

Just before nine o'clock, Kate parked in the crescent-shaped driveway in front of the enclave of businesses on La Brea. A single employee in the car rental agency was busily closing up; only the mail box rental office remained open at this hour. Kate trudged up the hill, examining again the path a killer or killers had taken to reach Dory Quillin.

'. . . *Break your head open you dyke bitch* . . .'

'. . . *Rearrange your face you motherfucker* . . .'

'. . . *Queerbashing asshole* . . .'

Other incoherent invective shouted by male and female voices reached her. Hurriedly she crested the hill and saw at the lighted windows of the Casbah Motel figures looking down into the parking lot. Adrenalin rushing through her, she ran toward the rear of the Nightwood Bar.

In orange light thrown by a single light standard more than a dozen women, including Maggie Schaeffer and Andrea Ross, formed a milling semi-circle around two youths, one muscular and black, the other white with greasy blond hair, both of them in jeans and tank tops. Brandishing lengths of thick pipe, they held Audie pinioned between them.

On the pavement in front of a black car with flames painted across its hood, Roz sat astride the writhing body of a third male, her smothering bulk squarely on his chest, her skirt thrown over his face.

Ash, Tora, and Raney, led by the shrieking Patton, surged toward the two youths who swung their weapons, howling curses; the women retreated, then gathered to move forward again — a wave swaying forward and back, its long dark shadow arcing across the parking lot in chaotic choreography.

'Police!' Reaching into her jacket for her gun, Kate pushed her way through the women, shoving the screaming Raney aside.

'Police!' She levelled her gun on the two men. 'Stop right there!'

'Fuck off!' Patton danced angrily in Kate's gunsights, waving her arms.

'Patton, get out of the way. *Now!*'

'Patton,' Maggie yelled, 'get the hell back here! All of you get out of the way!'

The wave of women swayed uncertainly, broke. The black youth holding Audie twisted her arm up behind her; Audie uttered a sharp cry of pain. Raney rushed past Kate; Kate grabbed her T-shirt and flung her aside. Raney staggered and fell to her hands and knees.

Patton yelled, 'Come on, let's *get* these creeps!'

'Move back!' Kate roared the command. 'Maggie, get these women back!'

'All of you *move*,' Maggie snarled, 'or you're eighty-six in this place till hell freezes over!'

Kate's eyes were fixed on the two young men who were pulling and dragging Audie backward with them toward their car; only Patton remained in a corner of her vision.

'Boys, stop right there,' Kate said in a calm voice. 'Listen to me. Drop the pipe now, nothing happens.'

'Sure,' the black youth sneered. 'You drop the gun, we drop the pipe.'

'Shoot their dicks off,' Patton shouted gleefully.

'Shut up,' Kate snapped. How to control Patton and defuse this situation without the use of force, without someone getting hurt?

'Patton,' Maggie yelled, 'shut your goddam stupid mouth and get back here!'

'Boys, drop the pipe,' Kate repeated, striding deliberately toward them. Choosing her man, she angled her wrist so that the thick black barrel of the .38 was at eye level of the blond youth.

His eyes, glassy and darkened by distended pupils, focused on her weapon. Audie jerked free of his grip, stumbled, fell to her knees. In the same instant, reacting with pure instinct,

Kate lunged bringing the handle of her gun down on the wrist of the blond. He dropped his pipe with a yowl of pain.

She caught the flash of movement; the black youth was swinging his weapon as Patton launched herself at him. Kate shoved the blond man with all her force into him. Both men crashed into the car.

Kate dug her gun into the throat of the black man. '*Drop it.*'

The pipe clattered onto the pavement.

'Face the car,' she hissed, glaring into his dark eyes. '*Now.*' Where was the other man? She couldn't spare an instant to look. She tensed, hunching her shoulders, knowing he was recovering his weapon.

As the black man turned she shoved him violently sideways. He stumbled along the side of the car, struggling to recover his balance. Yanking her handcuffs out of her bag, stuffing the gun into the belt of her pants, she grabbed his arm and clamped a cuff on one wrist. She dug the edge of the other cuff viciously into his spine. As he writhed she wrenched his other arm back and snapped on the remaining cuff.

Seizing her gun she leaped away from him and spun down into a defensive crouch, the gun raised and braced in both hands – and realized gratefully that Tora, Kendall, and Maggie had pinned the other youth over the car; his arms were raised to protect his head as Patton, leaping manically from side to side, beat on his arms with his own pipe. 'Gay-bashing asshole!' she shrieked.

'He's covered,' Kate shouted, 'everybody back!'

The women pulled away from the car except for Patton; Maggie grabbed her by the belt of her low-slung jeans and wrestled her aside.

Kate raised her voice: 'Somebody call me some backup.'

'I already have,' Andrea said from somewhere behind her.

The blond youth gained his balance, stared at Kate in glassy-eyed rage. He brushed at his arms and wrists as if to remove the blows he had received. 'Dyke,' he spat, leaning toward her, an arm loosely swinging.

'Stay right where you are.' Kate raised the barrel of her gun level with his face, knowing in despair that she might very well have to fire the weapon. He was a doper, he was mindless with drugs.

She heard sirens, the sound strengthening rapidly. Another minute, she needed to retain control for no more than another minute . . .

He stumbled toward her. 'You ain't got the balls to shoot, cunt.'

'Don't take another step.' Only a doper, unvulnerable with the courage of drugs, would not recognize his peril, would choose this moment when both of his friends were out of commission to make this suicidal move.

'Bulldykes, all of you —'

'Hi-yiih!' Patton shrieked, leaping to swing her pipe at his head.

In the same instant Kate seized and spun him, drove him forward and slammed him face down onto the hood of the car. Jamming the hard barrel of her gun into his neck, she put her face down next to his and screamed directly into his ear, 'Shut your mouth you *asshole* or I'll blow your head off!'

'Make me puke, dykes —'

All control left her. Rage poured through her, engulfing the adrenalin, choking her. 'You *slime*,' she screamed into his ear.

'Fucking dyke pig —'

Seizing his greasy blond hair she yanked his head up and then slammed his face into the hood of the car. She felt cartilage give way.

'My nose!' The voice was a high anguished scream. 'You busted my nose!' He broke from her grasp to paw in a frenzy at his face.

Kate backed away. The intense pain of a broken nose would break through even drug-induced armor.

'Police brutality, asshole,' Patton sneered. 'Big macho man, we'll all testify how this lady cop busted your nose, you no-balls asshole.'

With both men apparently incapacitated and backed up against the car, Kate kept her gun rigidly levelled on them. 'Roz,' she called, 'everything okay over there?'

'No problem.' Roz pulled her skirt from the face of her

captive, a beefy young male with stringy black hair and a face scarlet with impotent rage.

Maggie said breathlessly, 'We heard noise out here, they were trying to –'

'Later,' Kate ordered. She needed all of her concentration for the two men in her gunsights. 'And stay behind me.' Maggie had come up alongside her.

'Okay, sure.'

Shrieking sirens cut off on La Brea. Two black-and-whites climbed the hill, their lights cutting through the shadowed parking lot. Other sirens howled in the distance.

'Hey sister,' the black man called softly to Audie, 'we didn't figure you belonged here, we were just trying to get you away from these queers.'

'Of course.' Maggie stepped forward and bowed. 'Gentlemen like yourselves, you were politely forcing Audie into your scummy car and we were rude enough –'

'Hey sister,' the black youth said to Raney, his handcuffs clinking as he futilely jerked his arms, 'you my black sister, remember that.'

'You animal, who you calling a sister? These sisters are my sisters, you lowlife creep.'

Carrying shotguns, officers rolled out of their cars, Knapp and Hollings followed by Pierce and Swensen. Nodding to the officers, trying to conceal her relief, Kate replaced her gun in her shoulder holster.

Hollings cuffed the blond and patted him down, ignoring his blubbering about his nose. Pierce and Swensen walked over to Roz's captive and stood looking down at him, grinning.

'We'll take over from here, thank you ma'am,' Pierce said, and assisted Roz to her feet.

'Roll over, Beethoven,' Hollings ordered her captive, gesturing with the barrel of his shotgun, jingling his handcuffs.

Kate looked at Audie. She was huddled against Raney, her black face blank with shock, tears dripping from her eyes; she did not attempt to wipe them. Kate beckoned to Maggie. 'Take her inside, will you? You and Raney take care of her. Get everybody inside, I'll be right there.'

Officers had already escorted the black man to a police car. She said to Hollings, 'Keep them separate, make sure their rights are read to them. I'll get the full story here and be along.'

CHAPTER 11

Having seen all three prisoners taken away, Kate walked into the Nightwood Bar.

The women were gathered in a tight cluster, talking quietly, Audie in their midst as if in a protected center. Raney had an arm around her, watching with troubled eyes as Audie sipped from a steaming mug of coffee which she held in two trembling hands.

Kate searched out Andrea who nodded, her smile quick and warming. Kate made her way over to Audie and bent over the table to ask softly, sympathetically, 'Feeling any better?'

Audie nodded. 'Yes. Some. I do thank you, the way you helped, how you handled those filthy . . . those . . .'

'I didn't do it alone.' Kate straightened, spread both hands in a gesture that took in the entire group of women. 'I had this whole SWAT team to help – unarmed but very, very courageous.'

Maggie climbed to her feet and marched out from behind the table, her hands stuffed in the pockets of her lavender bermuda shorts. She shrugged one shoulder toward Kate and said gruffly, 'The woman did damn good by us.'

Patton also got to her feet to stand alongside Maggie. She had donned her yacht cap, apparently knocked off in the melee; now she doffed it in a grand sweeping gesture, bowing deeply toward Kate, and announced, 'Even I will concede that this woman's got ovaries.'

Laughing along with the women, Kate picked up a chair, carried it over to Audie's table.

'Those punks,' Maggie said, 'two of 'em white, one of 'em black. Ain't integration grand? We even have equal opportunity gangs.'

Audie, Kate noticed, was smiling with effort through the levity of her companions. Kate placed her chair opposite Audie and sat down, but addressed Maggie. 'What happened out there?'

'We heard racket.' Maggie gestured toward the parking lot. 'That souped up car of theirs – it sounded like bolts in a washing machine. So Patton and Roz went out. The three creeps had Audie –'

'Yeah,' Audie said, 'they –' Her shaking voice broke. Raney pulled her closer.

'They had Audie,' Patton put in. 'Trying to hustle her into their dumbshit macho car.' Her tone was withering in its contempt. 'We jumped the biggest asshole, we were yelling like banshees –'

'We all came pouring out there,' Kendall said, 'all of us –

'The dimwits grabbed the pipes outta their car,' Patton said, 'then you got here. Not that we couldn't handle those sleazy creeps ourselves –'

'But we still thank you anyway,' Maggie added wryly.

'Audie,' Kate asked softly, 'could we talk privately for a few minutes?' It was crucial now that she get Audie's individual story without embellishment or interference from the women – especially Patton.

Audie cast an alarmed glance at Raney, then at Kate, then back at Raney.

'Listen, it's okay, babe,' Raney said, 'the woman's okay. Let's get this over with.' Raney's long slender fingers were stroking the plump flesh of Audie's arm in a slow, soothing rhythm.

'I want you with me,' Audie whispered.

'By all means,' Kate told Raney.

A few moments later at a table in the rear of the bar, Kate said to Audie, 'I need you to answer just a few questions. Then, as soon as you feel strong enough, we'll go to the station –'

'No.' Audie shook her head and took a deep breath,

exhaled it in a sigh that took several moments to complete. 'I can't,' she said.

'Audie, try and relax. Just tell me exactly what happened. I promise I'll take good care of you, I'll —'

'You don't understand,' Raney said. 'She can't press charges and she can't testify.'

'I'm a kindergarten teacher,' Audie whispered. Tears welled, spilled down her cheeks.

'This is a lesbian bar,' said Raney. She gestured toward the rear of the Nightwood Bar, the parking lot. 'What happened out there happened at a dyke bar.'

Studying Raney's intelligent dark eyes, the handsome, chiseled face framed by the Grace Jones haircut, then Audie's round, motherly face, Kate remembered five novels she had read in college, books by Ann Bannon which Julie had loaned her while they were lovers. Those stories had been set in Greenwich Village in the fifties, when the great fear had been of police who periodically swooped down on gay bars to round up patrons, to permanently scar many of the lives of those patrons. . . .

'She can't press charges,' Raney said, and reached to Audie to tenderly brush strands of gray-threaded dark hair at her temple.

Kate fastened her gaze on Audie, who stared back at her out of dark eyes awash with tears. 'Audie, those three thugs who were here tonight — if they're allowed to roam the streets, they'll continue to prey on other gay people.'

Audie wiped her eyes with a sleeve of her cotton shirt, then placed both hands flat on the table. She sat up in her chair. 'I'm a black woman,' she said in a low, quavery voice. 'I know what goes on with the police and courts, I see it every day in my black neighborhood. What happened tonight — if I press charges and those three go to jail it's only for a little while.' Her voice rose. 'I have too much to lose, you hear? It's not *worth* it to me, you hear me?'

Kate nodded sadly. 'Yes, I hear you.' She added, 'But those men who were here tonight — has it occurred to you that they might have been here Sunday night as well?'

'No.' Audie stared at her. 'That's different. I can help

about Dory —' Her voice had lowered. 'If you find out they killed Dory —'

'Audie,' Kate said, 'it's not that simple. If you're willing to come forward, it has to be now. You have to file a police report right now, not after the fact. Otherwise a defense attorney would jump on any testimony from you with both feet. My own integrity and credibility as an investigating officer would be called into question. But if you do file a police report, I have to tell you it will be thoroughly investigated.'

Audie asked calmly, 'Their being here tonight — do you have any evidence about them besides that?'

'I can't discuss that with you,' Kate answered, softening her tone. 'But what went on here tonight is good evidence in itself. We'll know a lot more when we question them tomorrow.'

'They'll just deny everything,' Raney said. 'We know nobody saw Dory get killed.'

'Only one person swung that bat,' Kate replied, respecting the acuity of both these women under the circumstances. 'The other two may turn the killer in.'

'*May* isn't good enough,' Audie said with quiet emphasis.

'Their car,' Raney said, 'we'd have heard it Sunday night.'

'They could have used another car,' Kate countered.

'Why would they kill Dory?' Raney argued.

For kicks, Kate thought. *For no reason at all*. But these three dopers had been intent on taking Audie with them, and for obvious purposes. According to Patton, they had not even taken the pipes out of their car until the women came out of the bar. . . .

Suddenly tired, Kate rubbed her face with both hands. Still, a baseball bat had been used on Dory Quillin — and it was the same m.o. as a pipe. And how had the three known about this secluded bar? Why had they come here that Sunday night, maybe he had come back tonight with his buddies . . . Maybe. Maybe maybe maybe . . .

'What you're trying to do here is important, I know that,' Audie told her quietly, earnestly. 'I teach young black children — and my work is important too. To me and to them. From what you're able to tell me, with what I know — I'm sorry, the only decision I can make is no. I hope you can see why.'

'What I see,' Kate answered carefully, 'is a woman under the protection of the laws of this state who isn't exercising basic civil rights. But,' she conceded, 'I do also see your reasons.'

'I don't think there's any point in talking about this anymore,' Raney said. 'Audie's real upset, and I'd like to take her home.'

Tiredly, Kate nodded.

The three women rose, made their way to the front of the bar. 'Night guys,' Raney said to the group of women, 'Thanks again.'

Patton said to Kate, 'So now you know – Audie can't press charges. Maybe now you can see our whole problem with you as a cop. The people you're really protecting are heterosexual white middle class males and their female slaves.'

Kate fought down the surge of fury. Regardless of the inflammatory rhetoric, how could she not agree with the kernel of truth in what Patton had just said? From the hours she had spent in courtrooms she knew very well which class was the most adequately protected and defended.

She met Patton's pale blue eyes. 'All I can do as an individual police officer is try to make the laws of this country apply to everyone. And I think that's worth doing, I think it's worth trying to take from the streets creatures who don't deserve to live among human beings.'

She gestured at the group of women, her anger returning. 'But none of you will help yourselves or me. You tie my hands. It's not just tonight – it's everything. I'm trying to *help*. You wouldn't talk to me, any of you, the night Dory was killed. You won't do something as simple as help me find a woman I *must* talk to –'

'Wait,' Patton interrupted. 'Don't shit us, okay? You honestly think you can nail whoever did it to Dory?'

'I can only make every honest attempt I know how to make,' Kate answered. 'I've done that. I'll continue to do that.'

'We maybe haven't been too friendly,' Patton admitted, 'but we really don't know much more than we told you

Sunday.' There was an accompanying murmur of assent. 'We all liked Dory, we thought she was – she had something about her – she was special, that's all. But we didn't know her all that well, not even me, and I –' Patton broke off in apparent embarrassment; she drew the edge of a jogging shoe along a board on the floor. 'You really need to talk to Neely?'

'*Yes*.' Kate fixed her eyes on Patton as if to compel her with the intensity of her stare. 'I still have leads to check out, but I *must* talk to someone who knew Dory well, I have to get more current information about her life –'

'We'll do what we can,' Patton said.

'Yeah,' said Raney.

'Yes we will,' said Tora, her Hispanic accent liquidly musical.

Kate nodded, careful not to look at Andrea; instead she glanced at Maggie who answered with a faint but triumphant grin. Kate said to Audie, 'We'll do our best to make a few charges stick to those punks, regardless.'

But she had spoken out of a sense of needing to impart something positive to Audie for her trauma. Without corroborating witnesses and testimony, there was no case at all for assault and attempted kidnapping, or resisting arrest. Even a charge of disturbing the peace wouldn't stick. The best she could hope for was the presence of drugs in sufficient quantities on the three thugs or in their black Pontiac to bring felony charges. Otherwise they could only be held overnight for drug intoxication and questioning.

There was silence in the room; it felt awkward, and warm. 'Listen,' Kate said, 'the trouble here tonight is all over. It's early, why don't you all relax? I've got some punks I need to take care of down at the station.'

'Belly up to the bar, all you gutsy dykes,' Maggie called, striding to her post. 'This round's on the house.'

Their voices raised in animated conversation, the group of women broke up to head for the bar. Raney and Audie, an arm around each other, walked toward the front door.

Andrea joined Kate. 'I think I'll go on home as well.' Her face was tight, closed; she looked drained.

'I'll walk out with you,' Kate said, looking at her in concern.

At Andrea's car, a gray Olds Cutlass, Andrea turned, faced her. 'You have to get to your work,' she said in a tone of regret.

'Yes,' Kate said, also regretfully. 'Thank you for your help, for getting backup here so quickly.'

Andrea said in a sudden rush of words, 'I pass in the straight world, I pay the price – all the humiliation I can swallow, the jokes, the remarks –'

'I know,' Kate interjected.

'I realize there are crazy people out there who hate us to the point of murder. But to actually *see* that murderous hate, to come right up against it – it's like knowing about rape and then actually seeing it. And those sub-humans will get *away* with it . . . God,' she choked.

'Andrea,' Kate said in concern, 'do you have someone to stay with you tonight?'

'I'll be all right.' She gestured impatiently, looking away from Kate, her face closed again.

'Perhaps I could call you later?'

Andrea opened her bag, a large cloth affair with leather compartments, took out a case of business cards and a felt-tip pen, pushed up the sleeves of her oversize shirt, and leaned over the hood of her car. Kate watched her, thinking that Andrea seemed inordinately fond of oversize clothing.

'Yes, call,' Andrea said, giving her the card on which she had also written her address. 'If you feel like it, come over and I'll give you some coffee.'

'I'd like that,' Kate said softly. 'We won't be questioning those three till morning, so I won't be tied up for long.'

'Good.' Andrea opened her car door, slid behind the wheel. 'There's something I may want to tell you,' she said, and closed the door.

CHAPTER 12

Kate left the station shortly after ten o'clock. As she threaded her way through the downtown freeway interchange and over quiet city streets to the Silverlake District, persistent waves of fatigue encroached on her anticipation of time alone with Andrea. The day had been long, beginning with the autopsy of Dory Quillin and ending with the paperwork she had had to complete at the station. But it was the confrontation in the parking lot of the Nightwood Bar, the full expenditure of adrenalin, which had so depleted her.

The house was a small white frame, its old-fashioned veranda dark and shadowy with the shapes of leafy plants. Kate frowned at the flimsy aluminum-frame door, the light, easily removable screens and windows. A two-year-old could break into this place. Disturbed, she rang the bell.

From the backyard a dog snarled, then barked. Kate was suddenly bathed in light which illuminated the forest of plants on the veranda. To her relief, the light also revealed a substantial inside door and a barred living room window. The house was not nearly as vulnerable as it appeared.

Andrea, in jeans and a large blue plaid shirt, stood framed in the inner doorway, her house warm brightness behind her; then she came out onto the veranda to unlock the door. The rich aroma of coffee reached Kate. She felt suddenly weak with the womanly presence of Andrea and the warmth of her house; she ached with tiredness and loneliness.

'You look exhausted,' Andrea said, taking her arm, leading her into the living room. 'How about something stronger than coffee?'

'Coffee is fine.' Kate sank into a thickly cushioned sofa, and looked curiously around her. As if the veranda had overflowed into this room, plants occupied the floor and the slate hearth of a fireplace, as well as the surfaces of the glass-topped coffee table, two cherrywood occasional tables, several shelves of a tall bookcase. On the wall across from her hung a large print, geometric bands of color, costly-looking in its simplicity. The room had been put together with care, and Kate felt comfortable in it.

'Is it that you don't drink at all?' Andrea inquired. 'Surely you can't still be on duty. Do they work police officers eighteen hours a day?'

'On a homicide investigation we don't have set hours. We have to move fast, develop information fast. We go till we can't go any longer. So I'm still on duty. Technically, I have no business being here unless I *am* on duty.'

'Okay, you're on duty. Now what would you like to drink on duty? I have some excellent brandy, also scotch, vodka, wine – you look like a scotch drinker to me.'

Kate smiled. 'You're very observant. And kind. Right now some coffee with a little brandy sounds perfect.'

Andrea disappeared into the kitchen. Kate pulled an ottoman over from the end of the sofa, feeling at ease about doing so, and kicked off her shoes and put her feet up.

Andrea came back carrying two mugs of steaming coffee and placed them on the coffee table. From a cabinet in the bottom of the bookcase she took a bottle of Henessey and two bubble glasses, and poured generously.

'All the plants you have in here, they're wonderful,' Kate commented, accepting the snifter of brandy, warming it in both hands.

'Plants are easily the healthiest life forms on this earth,' Andrea said forcefully. 'They don't prey on one another, and you can keep them alive and growing forever.'

'I never thought about them that way,' Kate murmured, surprised by the intensity in Andrea's voice. The first sip of brandy was ambrosial, the liquor easing its silky way through her tiredness.

'Anything new on the three neanderthals?' Gracefully,

Andrea seated herself next to Kate, tucking her feet under her, her glass of brandy cupped in a palm.

'They all have rap sheets. Burglary, sale of stolen property. No drugs on them, there may be some in the car. But most dopers don't stockpile unless they're dealing, they can't afford to. They ingest whatever they buy.'

'Real assets to society,' Andrea said dourly.

Kate swallowed coffee that was strong and bracing. 'I can tell you what their story will be tomorrow when we question them. That Audie offered to go with them and you women at the bar interfered and I, prejudiced woman cop that I am, wronged them. We'll question them within an inch of their lives about Dory, of course.'

'Kate – young men like those three, surely they don't all end up in prison, there are too many. What happens when they grow up?'

'*If* they grow up,' Kate amended. 'Maybe one of the three –'

The phone rang. On the second ring it clicked into an answering machine.

'*Andy honey I know you're there, please pick up the phone* . . .' The woman's voice came softly from the speaker, tremulous with need. '*Andy . . . pick up the phone, baby . . . please* . . .'

Andrea walked over to the answering machine, turned the volume off. 'You were saying,' she said to Kate.

Kate swallowed more coffee. 'Maybe one of them will find a good person to marry,' she continued, watching Andrea as she settled herself once more on the sofa. 'But a felony record is death in the job market, and he'll never have a job of any consequence. Maybe he'll scratch along in the underground economy, maybe he won't.'

Andrea's eyes were fixed on the answering machine; its message-waiting light had not yet begun to blink, indicating that the caller was still speaking.

'More likely,' Kate continued, 'they'll all end up dealing drugs. Maybe get caught, do serious jail time. They'll probably die young – an overdose or a drug-related failure of some vital organ. Or their brains will get so fried they'll become wandering zombies living out of garbage cans.'

The message-waiting light finally began to blink, Andrea's eyes still fastened on it. Kate doubted that she had heard a single word she had said. 'Andrea,' she asked, 'is someone bothering you?'

Andrea's eyes, cool and expressionless, met hers. 'My ex-lover. She calls all the time. Thanks to my answering machine, I never have to talk to her.'

Her senses invaded by the subtle scent of perfume, the beauty of Andrea's face and bearing, Kate looked at her in a warmth of desire. Whatever could this ex-lover have done to earn such enmity from Andrea?

Kate cleared her throat. 'I was wondering, I thought perhaps . . .' She had spoken impulsively, and now she sorted through frantic thoughts: What could she invite Andrea to do? She was unable to cook a decent dinner, a movie seemed too juvenile. 'Depending on what happens with this case, I'm free this weekend. I thought perhaps . . . Maybe you'd like to have dinner at the beach —' She broke off, confused by the hardening grimness in Andrea's face.

'I was quite certain you were attracted to me.' The voice was flat, almost accusatory.

Confounded by Andrea's tone, Kate put down her coffee mug and tried to gather her wits. 'I — I'm sure I have that in common with a lot of women.'

'You're wasting your time, Kate.' The words were bitten off. 'I'm not at all what I seem.'

'In what way?' She was completely bewildered.

But Andrea did not reply. Closing her eyes, she lifted her brandy snifter and took a deep swallow.

'I go by instinct,' Kate said, desperate to bring this conversation into the realm of comprehension. 'I learned to do that in police work and I've relied on it — I've had to. You're one of the most interesting and attractive women I've met in a long time. In every way.'

'Every way,' Kate confirmed, still groping to locate solid ground somewhere.

Andrea seized the tails of her shirt in both hands and tugged it up and over her head.

Kate stared at two red scars making their jagged and

lengthy way across a puffy expanse of dusky flesh, the scars neatly and evenly cross-hatched by pink stitch marks.

'See how deceiving appearances can be?' Andrea's voice was soft; she did not look at Kate. She continued almost inaudibly, 'My breasts used to be larger than yours.'

Kate reached to her, needing to protect the rawness of those scars, needing to protect Andrea's nakedness from the coolness of this green room. She grasped Andrea's bare shoulders to warm her, rubbing, chafing the cool flesh under her hands, and looked into eyes that stared in amazement into hers.

'Listen to me,' Kate said quietly. 'The woman I loved burned to death a year and ten months ago. I would have taken her without arms or legs or breasts. I would have taken her with burns or scars or anything – if only Anne could have lived.'

Andrea buried her face in Kate's shoulder.

Kate took her into her arms, moved her hands over the soft flesh of Andrea's back. 'It's all right. Andrea, you're beautiful still. It's all right.'

'I'm not,' Andrea whispered. 'What Bev said was true.'

Bev – the woman on the phone? Andrea's former lover? 'What did she say?' Kate drew her close.

'Nothing. Nothing at all.'

'I don't understand. When was this?'

Andrea's voice was muffled against the fabric of Kate's jacket. 'Four months after . . . the surgery. I hadn't looked at myself, not even when the bandages came off. I . . . couldn't.'

Andrea lifted her head to gaze again at Kate, her brown eyes glistening with tears. 'I wouldn't let Bev look, either. We didn't make love, I was in pain some of the time, there was a lot of numbness . . . But mostly I couldn't stand to be touched. I felt so . . . *mutilated*. But I needed her to look at me, understand?'

'Yes,' Kate said.

'I had to have her do it for both of us and tell both of us it was okay, that it was okay for me to look at myself . . . understand?'

'Yes,' Kate said.

'And finally I did ask her . . . And then she didn't say

anything, she just stared at me and then I looked down and
I saw how hideous I was –'
'Andrea, you're still beautiful. You're a beautiful woman.'
Andrea shook her head. 'No. My breasts were *perfect* . . .'
She picked up her shirt, dabbed at her eyes.
'When did you have the surgery?'
'Six months ago.'
'Is everything okay? Are you fully recovered?'
'If you mean did they get it all, yes. The lymph nodes were
clear. They tell me I'll be fine.'
'How long were you and Bev together?'
'Four years.'
'You could have given her a little more time –' Kate sighed.
It was ludicrous, justifying the behavior of this woman she
did not know, whose turf she had just invaded.
'What you said, the way you – if only Bev . . .'
'Andrea, she had as much anxiety as you. Some people just
need more time to adjust. A friend of Anne's told her parents
she was a lesbian. They didn't take it well – but two months
later they were remorseful about how they'd reacted. Bev
sounded pretty remorseful on the phone.'
'Bev *is* slow to react about a lot of things, but this was
different, Kate. She *knew* about this. She knew days before
the surgery, all those months afterward . . .'
She had to convince Andrea, but to convince her she had
to defend Bev. And the more she defended Bev . . .
'Andrea, knowing about something like this doesn't matter.
I knew my mother was dying. But her actual death was a
shock I hadn't begun to imagine.'
Andrea was silent for some moments. 'I'm so sorry about
your lover,' she finally said. 'Anne was very lucky to have
you for the time that she did.'
'Thank you,' Kate said simply.
Andrea unbuttoned Kate's jacket, taking her time, and
pushed it off her. She slid her arms around Kate's shoulders.
'Your metal buttons are cold on my scars,' she said, smiling.
Kate chuckled, and picked up the shirt, draped it around
Andrea's shoulders. 'It's chilly in here.'
Andrea took Kate's face in her hands, looked into her eyes.
Kate's hands moved along the soft silky flesh of Andrea's

arms to her shoulders, down her back. She held Andrea's
eyes, knowing that with each passing moment Andrea saw
more and more clearly her desire.

'You're very beautiful.' Kate breathed the words; Andrea's
face was nearing hers.

'Stay with me tonight,' Andrea murmured against Kate's
lips.

Invigorated by cool sharp shower spray, Kate wrapped herself
in a towel and came into the small, dimly lit bedroom. Andrea
was propped up on pillows, her hair dark and glossy against
the whiteness, a sheet drawn up to her shoulders. She patted
the edge of the bed next to her. Smiling, Kate obediently sat
down beside her.

Andrea unwrapped the towel, dropped it to the floor, and
unhurriedly surveyed her.

'What a fine big woman you are,' she murmured, and took
Kate's face in her warm hands. She ran her fingers into Kate's
hair. 'Your hair is wonderful, so soft and fine . . .' Her fingernails stroked Kate's scalp, creating waves of chilling
sensation; Kate felt gooseflesh rise on her arms. Andrea's
hands came to Kate's neck, circling it, her palms exploring
its curving; then to Kate's shoulders, the nails again running
lightly; and Kate could not suppress her shudders.

Smiling in evident self-satisfaction, Andrea took Kate's
breasts in her hands, cupping them in her palms as if to weigh
them. She slid her palms around and around the curving of
them, and Kate closed her eyes to concentrate on the warm
friction, her sensations deepening as Andrea's fingers began
to sensuously knead, as a fingertip circled each nipple, then
stroked across it.

Andrea sat up and pushed away the sheet covering herself,
drew Kate to her. Again she took Kate's breasts in her hands,
this time to fit them into her, sighing as she sinuously adjusted
her own body. Kate slid her arms around the delicate slender-
ness of her, holding her closely, and lowered her slowly,
careful to preserve the melding of their bodies.

As Andrea's body joined the entire length of hers, Kate
sucked in her breath at the smooth warm silkiness of her.
Andrea's hands caressed down her back, the fingernails again

making her writhe; the warm hands moved over her hips, squeezing them with a proprietary roughness. Andrea's legs twined with hers; Kate felt the soft hair, the heat between Andrea's legs against her thigh.

'Your body is wonderful,' Andrea whispered, looking at her out of dark, heavy-lidded eyes.

Leaning on her elbows, she held Andrea's face in her hands, gazing at her, and stroked smooth firm skin that was like ocean-polished stone warm in the sun. Inhaling the scent of musk, her desire keenly penetrating, she whispered, 'God, I want you.'

Andrea pulled Kate's mouth down to hers, her lips a possessive, increasing pressure until Kate felt the impress of teeth; then Andrea's lips became sensuous softness, yielding under hers, and as Kate's tongue entered her Kate was freshly pierced by desire that ascended to an altogether new plateau.

Andrea's hands in her hair held Kate's mouth to hers, Andrea's tongue met hers with light swift strokes, Andrea's body became subtly undulant under hers. Kate felt the moist heat between Andrea's legs move against her thigh, felt herself go out of control for the second time this night. Overpowered by her craving, she slid a hand down to Andrea's thighs.

Her palm cupped exquisite mossy warmth, her fingers sank into a satiny depth; and Andrea's thighs closed powerfully, imprisoning her. Too fast, Kate thought amid the ecstasy of her sensations, I'm doing everything too fast. . . . But Andrea's mouth became pure passion under hers, Andrea tightened her arms around the thickest part of Kate's back and rocked her upper body against Kate's breasts. Then she buried her face in Kate's shoulder and opened her legs, her hips churning as Kate's fingers began to move. Soon Andrea's hips surged in what Kate thought was her coming until they surged again and again and again in a tense quivering that only gradually stilled.

'So good,' Andrea breathed, her body softening once more into Kate's. 'Oh God, so good.' Gently, she took Kate's hand away.

'Too fast, I was too –'

'I wanted you . . . God, just like that.'

She rolled Kate over onto her back and lay on top of her,

still breathing swiftly; Kate could feel her rapid heartbeats. Again Andrea fitted, adjusted Kate's breasts to her.

Kate saw the briefest wince of pain cross her face and asked in alarm, 'Did I hurt you? Was I too rough?'

Andrea took a shuddering breath, and smiled. 'Not that I noticed.' She added, 'Sometimes there's a little stinging around the scars – it's fleeting. They tell me it'll all be gone soon. Don't worry.' Andrea closed her eyes, nestled into Kate. 'You feel wonderful, your breasts are just incredible against me there.'

She held Kate's head cradled in her arms. 'You hardly need to apologize for anything,' she said, and kissed her.

With Andrea's mouth on hers in lingering tenderness, Kate explored the satiny body lying on hers, sliding her hands slowly over the curves of Andrea's back and the richly firm hips, down her thighs and under them, slipping a savoring hand again into the moist warmth between her legs. Andrea was tracing an ear with her tongue; her hand came slowly down Kate, her palm caressing over her stomach, to her legs. Kate squeezed her eyes shut against too much sensation.

Throbbing from wetly caressing fingers, groaning with her need, Kate put Andrea beneath her again and moved urgently, Andrea's fingernails raking across her shoulders, down her shoulder blades. Kate groaned again as the fingernails raced down her spine, and she arched, pressing into Andrea, transfixed.

Her release sweet and full, she took her body slowly, contentedly from Andrea, lassitude already permeating her. 'Don't let me sleep,' she murmured, 'I don't want to sleep.'

'I have other plans for you, you rough, tough cop. . . .'

Sometime later she lay helpless, her nipples a fiercely sweet ache in Andrea's mouth. Andrea's merciless fingernails seeming to be everywhere at once. Then Andrea's fingertips were stroking lightly between her legs, and then Andrea was under her again, fused to the needful rhythms of her body.

Exhausted, murmuring contentment, too utterly replete to struggle, she sank into sleep, Andrea warmly in her arms, Andrea's face pillowed against her breasts.

CHAPTER 13

She came out of dreamless sleep to Andrea's voice calling her name, and opened her eyes to the filtered light of an overcast morning framed between beige drapes.

Andrea, wearing an ice blue silken robe, sat gracefully on the end of the bed. She said gently, 'You told me last night you had to get up at six.'

Kate rubbed her eyes, alertness quickly returning; she felt rested, and possessed of a deep relaxation which she recognized as the aftermath of sexual release. She remembered the hunger, the haste of the night before, then the enervation and helplessness which had prevented her from exploring Andrea in all the intimate ways she had wanted. . . .

'I'm sorry I fell asleep on you, yesterday was just –'

'Will you please stop apologizing? I feel glorious this morning. You were completely and wonderfully satisfying to me.'

There was indeed a contentedness in Andrea's face, Kate realized, a tranquil beauty she had not seen before. And as if to confirm that she was a woman fully gratified, Andrea sat a distance from her on the bed, apparently not in need or in want of her touch this morning.

'I'm fixing some breakfast,' Andrea told her, smiling. 'Will you join me?'

'Coffee would be fine,' Kate said. Suddenly aware that she was ravenous, she added, 'And whatever you're having, if it's not too much trouble.'

'I eat toast and melon in the morning, will that be all right?'

'Fine,' Kate replied, longing for bacon and eggs and English muffins. Everyone she knew these days, except for Taylor, was eating food that was light, healthy, and, as far as she was concerned, depriving.

Andrea rose; her floor-length robe swirling about her feet, she made her elegant way from the bedroom. Kate took a quick shower, helped herself to deodorant, made do with mouthwash, and pulled on her clothes. She seated herself at the table in the dining alcove off the kitchen and cheerfully and swiftly polished off a third of a cantaloupe and two slices of whole wheat toast, declining seconds, having decided that she would have a decent breakfast later with Taylor.

Andrea was talking easily about the changes she had made in this house since buying it two years before, and her pride and pleasure in it. There was a formality about her that Kate sensed she should not disturb; and she responded with anecdotes of her own experience as a homeowner, careful not to allude in any way to their communion in the night.

Then Andrea said, spearing her last chunk of cantaloupe, 'I was never unfaithful to Bev the whole time we were together. Do you believe that, Kate?'

'Of course I believe it,' Kate said, finishing her coffee. 'I was never unfaithful to Anne and we were together twelve years.'

Andrea smiled. 'Yes, I can sense you'd be like that with a woman you loved. But after the way Bev was about my surgery . . . I don't care how many times she tried to explain, or what she did or said, she could never have been the first woman in my bed after my operation, do you understand that?'

'I still think you're being a little hard on her,' Kate answered, refilling her coffee cup, not caring a whit about Bev.

'I was in the Nightwood Bar waiting for you,' Andrea said softly. 'I didn't know how long I'd have to continue going there till someone like you came in. Women approached me, but I was waiting for you. Just you.'

Kate stared at her, amazed and speechless. Andrea, regal in the clinging silkiness of the blue robe, had never seemed more beautiful to her.

'Maybe I willed you to me because of my need,' Andrea

mused her dark eyes distant. Then she looked candidly at Kate. 'I needed a woman I admired and respected, a woman who was not just attracted to me, but who *I* found attractive, too.'

'Thank you,' Kate managed.

'No. I'm the one who owes all the thanks. For the first time in my life I needed validation as a woman. And I had to have it from you. Not from Bev, not from just any woman, but from you. When you wanted me last night and made love to me the way you did, you were everything I needed.'

Kate looked at her in quiet wonder.

Andrea continued in a sober tone, 'And I enjoyed pleasing you, I enjoyed you, Kate.'

A silence fell between them that was delicate, cocoon-like; Kate felt unwilling to disturb it. She drank her coffee as Andrea glanced into a leather-bound appointment book presumably listing her real estate activity for this day.

Finally, Kate rose. Andrea took her arm, walked with her to the door.

Her hands gentle on Andrea's shoulders, Kate kissed her forehead. 'I'll call you as soon as I can,' she said. 'Will you be here this evening?'

'Of course.'

Something about the tone rang oddly to Kate's ear; she looked sharply at Andrea. But Andrea was smiling.

Kate sat at her desk in the Detectives Squad Room looking over the notes of her separate interrogations of the three young men arrested at the Nightwood Bar.

Perry Jerome Lee, the black youth, appeared to be solidly alibied; on Sunday afternoon and evening he had been in South Central L.A. playing pool in Jakey's Bar; he claimed two bartenders would vouch for him. Robert Kenneth Johnson and Gerald Thomas Petrie had been 'just hanging out' and could not or would not account for their specific whereabouts. Lee and Johnson had come to the Nightwood Bar at Petrie's suggestion; Petrie, who lived in a furnished room on Sycamore, had heard 'around the neighborhood' that there had been a death at 'this weirdo bar for dykes' and wanted to 'take a look at this weirdo joint and its weirdo customers.'

From there the stories diverged. Lee had been merely 'trying to rescue a black sister, she had no truck at all with those perverts.' Johnson and Petrie's story was as Kate had foretold: Audie had agreed to accompany them, and first the women and then Kate had interfered. In Kate's presence Petrie had only once touched the bridge of his nose and the bruising along his cheekbones, then jerked his hand away; he did not mention his injuries.

According to Petrie and Johnson, they'd maybe had a few drinks, nothing more. Lee claimed with a straight face that he had accepted pain pills from a friend for a headache. The Pontiac had checked out clean. . .

During her intense questioning of each of the three, Taylor had been present but merely listened, a foot propped up on the interrogation room table, his silent, ominous presence drawing increasingly uneasy glances from each youth. Now Taylor was taking his own turn with them, working solo, bringing the suspects back one at a time to point up the contradictions in each of their stories.

Kate tossed her note pad onto the desk. Petrie – or perhaps both Johnson and Petrie – could be involved with Dory Quillin's death, but instinct told her it was unlikely. They were both petty thieves and dopers, and the money and cocaine in Dory Quillin's van had been left intact. Thieves could indeed be rapists, but they seldom crossed over into gratuitous killing. In any case they would have to be released; there was nothing to hold them on.

Amid the hum of conversation, the slamming of file drawers, the usual buzzing activity of the drab Squad Room, Kate heard her name over the paging system. She picked up her phone. 'Detective Delafield.'

'This is Neely Malone.' The voice was high and soft. 'I'm sorry, I've known for a few days that you wanted to talk to me, but I haven't been in any condition to talk to anyone since Sunday night.' The words were spoken tremulously, but with the precision and enunciation of a well-educated woman.

'Miss Malone, I understand,' Kate answered, her elation at

finally contacting this woman evaporating in sympathy for her grief. Whatever role Neely Malone had played in Dory Quillin's life, hers was the first emotion she had sensed in anyone that seemed deeper than transitory mourning. 'I'm truly sorry for your loss.'

'Thank you. Thank you for your understanding. From what I hear about you, I know you do understand.'

Apparently the women at the Nightwood Bar had conveyed their trust in Kate, or their knowledge that she was a lesbian, or both.

'My partner and I would like to talk to you. Would it be convenient –'

'It would be convenient for me to come there,' Neely Malone said with polite firmness. 'Would eleven o'clock be all right?'

'We'll see you then, Miss Malone.'

At ten-thirty Taylor sauntered back into the Squad Room and slid a hip onto the edge of Kate's desk. He chuckled, and aimed a playful punch at her shoulder. 'Petrie got real pissed when I asked about the marks on his face. Said it was none of my fucking business that he got in a scuffle with some dude – *dude*, you got that? – *before* he got to the Nightwood Bar.'

Kate smiled wryly. 'Is that a fact?' Audie had refused to press charges because she was a lesbian, and now one of Audie's assailants refused to claim excessive force – or to acknowledge any force at all – by a police officer because that officer was a woman.

'Taking on three assholes loaded on drugs, you should get a medal,' he growled. 'It *bugs* me we gotta let 'em go, Kate. They'd have taken that woman and raped her out of her mind, they're pure dogshit, you can *smell* 'em.' Taylor was jerking a contemptuous thumb repeatedly toward the interrogation room. 'What *really* bugs me is Petrie. If he wasn't too much of a macho man to admit he got taken down by a woman cop, you'd be in a hassle right now with Internal Affairs. *That's* the shit that makes me want to grab the goddam twenty-year pension and go raise goddam avocados.'

Kate succumbed to his angry cynicism, adding to it her

own vindictiveness: Petrie deserved much more than just getting his face smashed into the hood of a car. All three of the creeps did.

Yet, in the cold, objective core of her she knew she had been out of control in that parking lot. A police officer must always perform with poise – and while she had used force out of necessity, her rage as a lesbian woman had also been a major component. Just as well she did not have to explain and defend herself to Internal Affairs.

'Ed, those three aren't so dumb they can't figure out why they weren't booked. They'll go back up to that bar –'

Taylor crossed his arms. 'I made a few suggestions to the three gentlemen.'

Kate grinned at him, knowing the tone, imagining him in the interrogation room, his bulk looming over each suspect, his face close to theirs as he spoke softly, politely. Taylor at his most polite was Taylor at his most menacing.

'So tell me, Ed.'

'I strongly suggested to Mr. Lee and Mr. Johnson that unless we have further questions for them about Sunday's events at the Nightwood Bar, two-bit hoods like themselves should think very carefully before coming back into this division, that we would not be nearly so gracious and hospitable next time. I suggested to Mr. Petrie in particular that since he continues to smell up our division by living here, if he's so hard up that he needs to go looking for lesbians, maybe his manhood needs further research – and the next time we pick him up I'll see to it personally that he gets put in a certain detention cell where his masculinity will be thoroughly and exhaustively researched.'

Laughing, sitting back in her chair with her hands behind her head, Kate said, 'Ed, by all means let's requisition that detention cell.'

'The assholes,' Taylor pronounced in final dismissal. 'So what's on the agenda for today, Wonder Woman?'

'Neely Malone will be here in a few minutes. Depending on what she tells us, we may have new leads to check out. Otherwise we finish up Dory Quillin's john list.'

Taylor groaned loudly.

'Then we pick up a gasoline credit card for a trip tomorrow to interview the ex-gym teacher in Modesto.'

Taylor groaned even more loudly. 'Hours and hours of nothing but looking at farmland and cows. Coming and going. Shit, Kate.'

Neely Malone sat in the straight-backed chair in the interrogation room and passed a hand over a modest and perfectly round afro with a streak of gray through it like the flange on a Roman helmet. Then she removed rimless glasses, reached into her purse and extracted a tissue and dabbed at her red-rimmed eyes, and replaced the glasses.

She looked at Kate. Her dark eyes, accented by a touch of burnt sienna eyeshadow and magnified by the thick lenses, seemed propelled out from her round face. 'Please call me Neely,' she said in the high, soft, tremulous voice Kate had heard on the phone.

She was a rotund woman, her generous curves enhanced by her flowing, casual clothing. Kate liked the maroon tunic, the clay-colored loose trousers of very light crinkled cotton; the colors were rich against the honey-brown tones of her skin. But it was Neely Malone's magnified eyes that were most arresting: they confirmed the intelligence Kate had heard on the phone, and they contained unmistakable softness and compassion. She appeared to be a woman of great warmth and givingness, and Kate was instinctively drawn to her.

Taylor came into the room, Kate introducing him as he settled in next to her at the blond formica table. 'Ma'am,' he said, 'we've very sorry, and sorry to have to trouble you.'

Taylor's approach was unusually deferential, even to a tearful woman; and Kate saw that he was disconcerted. The motherliness of Neely Malone obviously did not fit into any of his stereotypical concepts of lesbians. She said to Neely, 'Perhaps we could start by having you tell us when you last saw Dory.'

'A week ago today. She came over for dinner. She called the next night, and that was the last . . .' She dabbed under her lenses with her tissue, then took the glasses off and tucked them away in her purse. 'She dropped in for dinner whenever the spirit moved her, I was always glad to have her. She went her own separate way from me ten months ago.'

The words had been spoken calmly, without bitterness; there was no attempt to cover up who had left whom. Kate studied her a moment longer before asking, 'How long did you know her altogether?'

'She lived with me not quite eleven months. I met her almost exactly a year before that, I —'

'So you knew her from the time she was what, seventeen?' Kate interrupted, wanting to complete these figures in her notes before Neely continued.

'Only in a manner of speaking. I was going to say I met her for the first time at USC County General. I'm a nurse, I work graveyard in the psychiatric ward.'

Neely intercepted Kate's glance of amazement. 'Drugs,' she said succinctly. 'She did cocaine mixed with God knows what, I don't remember, heroin in all probability. She went beserk, they brought her in in restraints. Young people, they put any sort of junk into themselves, the stories I could tell you . . .' She raised her hands in a gesture of futility. 'The drugs she took brought her to some terrible, terrible place.'

Her eyes were distant, narrowing with the pain of memory, filling with tears that spilled over. 'That night I held her as much as I could, restraints and all, and talked to her. It did seem to help. Her poor little body jerked and twitched, she was moaning so . . .' Neely paused to swab the tears from her cheeks. Kate could easily imagine her plump figure in a white starched uniform, could visualize her bringing comfort to the agonized Dory Quillin with her warmth and calm, motherly strength.

Neely shook her head vigorously, as if to cleanse it of memory. 'Sometime that next day she straightened out — or at least she was gone from the ward my next shift. The next time I saw her was a year later. I broke up with a lover and went out to the bars again, and I saw her at the Horn — that's a club in the Valley that draws older, more established women. I learned later that she needed a mature woman, someone she could trust. She was eighteen by then, and of course I'd had no idea she was gay. I didn't think she would possibly remember me – but she did. She came home with me that night, and didn't leave.'

'During that time –' Taylor cleared his throat; Kate knew he was phrasing his question with care. 'During that time she wasn't doing drugs or . . . plying her other trade?'

'Wrong,' Neely said crisply. 'She still did coke once in a while. But selling her body – that happened much more often.'

'Did it bother you?' Taylor asked.

At least once every interview, Kate thought in disgust, Taylor had to be an idiot at least once every interview.

'Bother me?' Neely uttered the words as if examining excrement. 'Would it bother you if your wife was a hooker?'

Taylor, writing in his notebook, did not reply. Neely spoke directly to Kate. 'She couldn't see why selling her body to men mattered, even to someone who loved her. Because it meant nothing at all to her. Her body was a commodity attached to nothing else about herself, she could sell it at a good price – so why not? And you couldn't convince her it was degrading because she was so totally contemptuous of her johns that she thought they were the ones who were degraded.'

'Eleven months,' Taylor said. 'If she was so hopeless, why'd you stick with her even that long?'

'She wasn't hopeless. And while I was trying to help her I grew to love her very much,' Neely said simply, and Kate believed her.

Neely continued, 'I had to be extremely careful with any attempt to change her behavior. It was all a matter of approach, of challenging her. I accused her of abandoning school because she lacked the courage to continue. That infuriated her, she went out and passed the high school equivalency test, she enrolled at L.A. City College.'

'She ever attend classes?' Kate asked, smiling at Neely's deviousness.

'She took introductory courses in psychology, sociology, and philosophy,' Neely said proudly. 'I've still got the text-books, her notebooks too. She'd just enrolled for –' She broke off; her eyes teared again.

'Neely,' Taylor said, 'why did she leave you?'

She reached into her purse for another tissue. 'Everything fell apart when Mama had her stroke. It was a terrible time, I had terrible money worries . . . All of a sudden between my job and worrying over Mama I had almost no time to give Dory. . . .'

Neely blew into her fresh tissue. 'Then what happened was even worse. Mama's medical bills were just –' Neely gestured with a palm extended high over the floor. 'Dory offered money. Twenty-eight hundred dollars cash, most of it hundred dollar bills. I couldn't take it – I couldn't. Because I knew how she got it and – I mean, how could I take that kind of money from her, how could I?'

Neely blew her nose again. 'I've had psychological training, I knew why children become prostitutes, I knew the pattern of Dory's life, I *knew* not to be judgmental or punitive because that's exactly what she'd run away from. But that's what she saw.'

'Excuse me,' Taylor said, getting up. The door of the interrogation room was ajar, and Taylor was being paged.

'Please go on,' Kate said to Neely.

'I knew Dory would leave someday, I knew that. But she needed caring for, and safe shelter until she was ready . . .' Neely shook her head. 'Anyway, she bought her van and that was that. I thought the Nightwood Bar wasn't the worst place for her to stay. Maggie's a good woman, I knew she was keeping an eye on her. I didn't go there except once in a while, I had to let my wounds heal.'

'Neely, do you have some notion of what her current life was like, her associates? Whether she had any enemies?'

'Enemies?' Neely shrugged. 'You know maybe even better than I do how dangerous it was – that young girl with those strange men. But she never talked about them, except to laugh and sneer. Whenever she came over to see me she talked about women she met at the bars, or about her classes, or books . . . And of course her parents. I assume you know all about *that*.'

Kate said carefully, 'We've been trying to put together an objective picture of Dory's life, but they haven't been too helpful.'

Neely smiled faintly. 'I imagine not. A couple of weeks

after Dory was with me she claimed they wanted to meet me. The little liar,' she murmured, smiling softly as she remembered. 'She claimed they knew she was a lesbian, and of course by then I didn't have nearly enough of a picture of her life with them to know everything that was going on . . . so it was a bizarre new version of guess who's coming to dinner, except we got only as far as the living room. Her father ordered us out, I thought her mother would have a heart attack. I was mortified.'

Neely erased any impression of mortification with a chuckle so infectious that Kate responded to it with a grin of her own. 'I was so furious with Dory,' Neely reminisced, 'but later I understood why she did it — she wanted to force her mother to face reality just once, to see and to *believe* something about her.'

Taylor had returned to his chair, and Neely addressed both detectives: 'You do know her father molested her?'

'Neely,' Kate said, 'we really can't discuss the information we've put together. But we'd like to know anything you can tell us about that.'

Neely said quietly, 'If I'd known about Roland Quillin before I met him, I'd have vomited all over him. And Flora Quillin too. With all her denying, she's just as bad. Both parents denying even the *existence* of the damage they'd done —'

'Do you think,' Taylor asked, 'or did Dory think they were responsible for her turning out the way she did?'

Neely winced at the question, then said forcefully to Taylor, 'What do you think? They denied sexual abuse, they rejected her as a lesbian, as a person —'

'So why didn't she just reject them right back? If they were my parents I'd have told 'em exactly where to get off.'

'No way,' Neely said heatedly. 'You're telling me you could just walk away if someone committed a crime against you?'

Fat chance, Kate thought.

'Dory couldn't walk away from that any more than you could. She *couldn't* have them not matter to her, she was obsessed with extracting some kind of acknowledgment from them.'

Then Neely's shoulders slumped, and she sighed. 'She even

114

took it into her head to sue. And she was serious.' She said to Taylor, 'Imagine thinking you could sue six years after a crime, when you've already accused an innocent teacher of a similar crime, when you've concealed from a psychologist what really happened, when you've been making your living as a prostitute.'

'Not a chance,' Taylor said.

'Exactly what I told her.'

'This business with the father,' Taylor said, tapping his pen on his note pad. 'If she made it up about the teacher, then why not the father?'

Neely Malone fixed her dark eyes on him. 'She could have sex freely with men she despised, but when it came to lovemaking she really wanted – she froze. I happen to have first-hand knowledge. She told me what he did to her, but I knew anyway because of what she couldn't bring herself to do with me. First he'd fondle her between her legs, then he'd masturbate while he was performing cunnilingus on her. During school term he did it whenever he could get her alone away from her mother. During summer vacations he did it daily, sometimes several times a day. And he did it from the time she was five.'

Kate felt as if she were caught in a pool of silence containing only herself and Taylor and Neely Malone. Finally she said, 'Dory took a trip up to Central California a few days before she –' She fumbled for words. '– before it happened.'

'I know,' Neely said. 'Or at least I know she went somewhere. She called last Thursday night, she had something to do up north, she'd be over to see me with some news soon after she got back. I remember she sounded very quiet on the phone, kind of strange, and I asked what was wrong, where was she going. She just repeated what she'd already said.'

'Do you think she might have gone up to see the teacher she accused?'

'Him? I don't believe she ever knew where he ended up. But maybe she found out, maybe that's exactly where she went. To see him, explain. It never stopped bothering her, you know.'

From a folder on her desk Kate extracted and held up a photocopy of the figures she had found in Dory Quillin's van.

S285
S288
S290

'Does this mean anything to you?'

Neely glanced curiously at the figures. 'No. Should it?'

'We believe Dory was working on this shortly before . . . the time of her death.'

Neely reached for the paper, spread it over her lap. A tear splashed onto the page. 'Oh my God, look what —'

'It's all right,' Kate said. 'Take your time, Neely.'

'I can see Dory was agitated . . . The numbers look so . . . powerful,' she murmured. She examined the figures for some time. 'I have no idea what it means,' she finally said. Running her fingers over the paper, she asked huskily, 'Could I possibly have this to keep?'

'Of course.'

Kate watched Neely's hands fold the paper and tuck it carefully in the side pocket of her purse, the hands large and capable and yet soft-looking, the hands that had held and loved Dory Quillin. . . .

'Thank you for your help,' she said, thinking that while Neely had succeeded in bringing the dead young woman with the blonde hair and silver-blue eyes more fully to life for her, Neely had brought her no closer to finding Dory Quillin's killer. Leads had now reached the vanishing point.

Again Taylor was paged; with a mutter of apology he trudged from the room to answer his phone.

'Do you know —' Neely's voice faltered. 'The Quillins, do you know what arrangements they've made about . . . Dory?'

'No I don't,' Kate answered softly. If the Quillins felt no obligation to identify their daughter's body, would they wish to claim it for burial?

'Dory loved the water so,' Neely whispered. 'I know she'd want her ashes scattered at sea. Do you think you could get the Quillins to do that? Or to maybe release the body to me? I'd find the money somewhere, I'd just have to.'

'I don't know,' Kate said. 'Neely, I'll see what I can find out.'

'I've been thinking the past three days and nights why I loved her so much,' Neely said. 'I know part of it was because there was so much child in her, so much mother in me. She was the child I always wanted – in my day you couldn't have a child and live as an independent lesbian like some of us do today. But Dory was every bit a woman, too, and so beautiful, you know . . . Smart as a whip, bright and quick . . . and sweet and tender . . . One minute she'd be arguing over some passage in her philosophy book, the next minute she'd be crying over a dead bird she found in my garden. She was awkward as a colt in some ways, you just wanted to hug her all the time. There's a phrase from somewhere in Shakespeare I remember from high school, it's been running through my mind these past days – "Life's bright fire."'

Aching with sympathy for the woman across from her, Kate sat quietly, unmoving, while Neely dabbed again at her eyes.

'Most of us are gray people who just make our way through life,' Neely said. 'And then some of us are like Dory. I know she's what Shakespeare thought about when he wrote that phrase – she *was* life's bright fire.'

Gently, Kate said the words Andrea had spoken last night about Anne: 'She was lucky to have you for the time that she did.'

Neely Malone nodded, put her glasses back on, gathered her purse, and rose. She took the card Kate handed to her, then looked at the case file on the table, at the yellow pad with Kate's notes of this interview. 'To be filed away in the records of a police station – I guess that's more immortality than most of us will ever have.'

CHAPTER 14

As Kate and Taylor left the station to check out the remaining names on Dory Quillin's john list, Taylor was whistling cheerfully. Kate knew the reason for his good humor: there were only these last interviews to conduct, the trip to Modesto tomorrow, and then the basic investigation of the Dory Quillin homicide would be complete. The case would begin its inexorable fade into pseudo life, the file proceeding through a review process beginning with Jake Belliard, the D-3 in charge of the homicide table, and involving Lieutenant Burke and other superior officers; then it would be relegated to limbo – to a permanent open file containing all unsolved homicides, to be granted conditional life only during periodic review and when its basic data, entered in computer files, matched a new and similar crime.

She was not consoled by the fact that unsolved cases were a small percentage of homicides overall, that most persons who died at the hands of another were victims of someone they knew, and that competent and careful investigations inevitably led to arrests and convictions. Unable to distract or soothe herself even with thoughts of Andrea, she glared out the window of the Plymouth, struggling to conceal her rising anger at Taylor.

His attitude toward an unsuccessful investigation could always be plotted on a predictable curve: as his hope waned, so did his interest. He did everything necessary – after all, no obvious stone could be left unturned when a major crime case file was subject to close supervisory scrutiny – but he went through the motions, carried out his duties with minimal competence, his mental machinery operating in low gear. And an uninterested detective, she raged, could miss possibilities, could miss subtleties and nuances that suggested new leads. . . .

As Taylor, whistling 'Country Roads,' drove them through the smog and overcast, through the clogged auto and pedestrian traffic of downtown L.A., she maintained her baleful silence.

All the interviews were located in office buildings within a ten block area around Seventh and Flower Streets, and by early afternoon she and Taylor had reached the final entry on Dory Quillin's list.

Pembroke Investments, Inc. occupied the eighth and ninth floors of an office building on Flower. The spacious ninth floor office of securities analyst Gabriel Koerner had a view, albeit distant, of delicate white buildings on a green hilltop – the graceful Grecian architecture of the Music Center. Despite the presence of three phones on Koerner's desk – a conventional instrument and two large consoles with constantly flashing lights – the office seemed quiet, almost hushed. Koerner's eyes, Kate noted, darted constantly to the two consoles.

Koerner was small and thin, with sandy hair which had receded substantially; he was in his early thirties, perhaps younger. He wore a gray satin-backed vest unbuttoned over a white shirt with the sleeves rolled to the elbows; his loosened maroon-striped tie hung with its tails askew. In sharp contrast to the guarded, resentful reception of the other men on Dory Quillin's list, he had welcomed the detectives with a smile and friendly handshake, waving them to the two leather armchairs in front of his desk.

'Sorry to disturb you, I see this is a busy day,' Kate said as she sat down, seeing his eyes shift once more to the consoles.

He chuckled. 'No, just one hell of a busy morning.' He glanced down as if remembering his attire, and tightened the knot of his tie, began to button his vest. 'The market's closed, I'm still decompressing.' His voice resonated with energy and optimism. 'What a morning, another big move in the Dow. If you two aren't playing the market you should be.'

Taylor said drily, 'I happen to have a spare twenty.'

119

'Fifty thousand's our usual –' Koerner's blue eyes scanned Taylor's polyester jacket and pants. 'Yeah, well. . . .' He finished buttoning his vest and then gave Taylor a wary smile. 'So how can I help you?'

Koerner cast the merest flick of a glance at the photo Kate placed on his leather-topped desk. 'Dory Quillin.'

Kate looked at him sharply. To the other men on the list the woman in the photo had been merely 'Dory' – if they mentioned a name at all.

'Yeah,' Koerner said, 'I heard you were asking questions.'

'Who told you?' Taylor commanded.

'Dickie Fishlin,' Koerner said immediately and agreeably.

Kate thought back. Fishlin had been perhaps their sixth or seventh interview; he had said nothing unusual, had been neither more nor less cooperative than anyone else.

'Dickie told me about her maybe a year or so ago, said she was . . . Look, I've got nothing to hide, not a thing.' He raised his hands palms up and offered an easy smile. 'Sure I met her. Sure I knew what she had for sale. But nothing happened. In fact, it was just the damnedest thing. . . .'

He swung around to his credenza, poured pale yellow liquid from a crystal pitcher into a matching crystal glass. 'Pineapple juice,' he explained. 'Can I get you both something? Some of this? We have coffee out there,' he added, inclining his head toward the closed office door as if toward a place he disdained.

Both detectives shook their heads. 'Thank you,' Kate added. Taylor's arms were crossed; he was eyeing three silver sailing trophies on Koerner's credenza.

'I drink this stuff all the time. No coffee, no drugs, a drink or two at night, that's it. Don't smoke, don't allow it in here, either. Who needs it? Having a stock do what you've told investors it'll do, if there's any bigger –'

'Why was your meeting with Dory Quillin the damnedest thing?' Taylor interrupted, flipping open his notebook. Kate could see that he detested Gabriel Koerner.

'Because I knew her only about five minutes. And it was one weird five minutes. I can tell you every single word we said to each other. I met her in the bar at the Bonaventure last Thursday night at seven o'clock.'

Kate stared at him, dismayed. Why had it not occurred to her that the last man – the newest man – on Dory Quillin's list might also have been the last to see her alive?

'At ten after seven, I should say. I was on time, she was late. Her name was Dory and she'd be wearing white – that's all I knew. And then in she comes and I tell you she was . . . well, Dickie said she – I mean, she was a knockout. White pants, a white silk shirt, young, blonde, slim as a pencil, I didn't really believe it when Dickie told me, but – I still can't believe she turned up dead just three days later. Somebody killed her, right?'

'Correct,' Taylor said in a tone that forbade further questions.

Koerner shook his head, picked up his crystal glass. 'So anyway she sits down, I'm still catching my breath. I say hello, how are you, and then I suggest dinner at the hotel.' He drained his juice, looked brightly at the detectives. 'They have this terrific restaurant –' He broke off, apparently seeing something in Taylor's face. 'Then the cocktail waitress is right there wanting to know what the young lady would like to drink. She orders a tall vodka and tonic, and the waitress asks for ID which I can't blame her for.'

With his eyes averted Koerner picked up the photo of Dory Quillin lying on his desk and handed it to Kate. 'Put this away, okay? Anyway, she gets out her wallet and shows it to the waitress and then she says something else about her drink, wanting something in it beside lime – I forget. Her wallet's lying open on the table, so I take a look at her driver's license, curious, you know? And I see her last name is Quillin.'

Koerner turned around, poured more pineapple juice; Taylor glanced at Kate, rolling his eyes in disgust.

Koerner said, 'Quillin is kind of an uncommon name, you know, so I tell her I remember a Quillin from years ago in my home town. But this Quillin was not such a terrific guy – he got run out of town for molesting little girls.'

Kate sat up abruptly in her chair.

'When was this?' Taylor exclaimed.

Kate recovered herself. 'Ed, let him finish his story first. Then what happened, Mr. Koerner?'

'Christ what's going on here? You two look as shocked as she did. She asked where I was from and I told her Summerville – that's a little town on the outskirts of Fresno.'

Fresno. In Central California. . . .

'So then she wants to know about the little girls, what all that was about. Hell, I couldn't remember all that much, it was twenty-some-odd years ago, you know? I was like nine years old. This Quillin guy'd been operating in Kennedy Memorial Park, he molested I don't know how many little girls before they caught him.'

Quillin was arrested. And booked. . . .

'Paula Jankowski, she was one of them, she lived right down the block from me. Her parents were old country Polaks, they wouldn't let her go near a courtroom. But Paula's father – hell, I'm getting ahead of myself. Anyway, this Quillin guy goes on trial in Fresno – that's the county seat –'

He was prosecuted, there was a trial record. . . .

'Nearly as I can remember there was all kinds of commotion with the parents about the little girls testifying.'

Kate thought: How could I have been so *stupid* not to recognize Dory's numbers? Me of all people – how could I have been so goddam *stupid*?

As Koerner paused to drink more juice, Taylor asked, 'Do you know this Quillin's first name?'

Koerner shook his head. 'She asked me too. I can't remember.'

'Ever see this guy?'

'She asked me that, too. Nope, I just heard all kinds of stories, it was all the town talked about that whole summer.'

'How about a picture of him in the paper?'

Again Koerner shook his head. 'This was 'sixty-four, don't forget. Stuff like that didn't get headlines like all this McMartin pre-school business today. I don't remember – either the guy was acquitted or maybe the parents wouldn't go through with having their kids testify – but he got off. And that's when Paula's father met the guy outside the courtroom and laid his face open before anybody could drag him away.'

The scar on Roland Quillin's cheekbone. . . .

'Quillin took the hint and hightailed it out of town,' Koerner concluded.

Taylor asked, 'How did Dory Quillin react when you told her all this?'

'Took off running like those white clothes were on fire. And that was the last I saw of her. Christ was I embarrassed. The people in that bar looked at me like –'

'Mr. Koerner,' Kate said, 'is there anything else you can add to what you've told us? Anything else Dory Quillin said? Or did?'

Koerner shook his head to each of the questions. 'Nope, that's it. That's everything I know.'

Kate nodded to Taylor, and rose. 'We'll want a formal signed statement from you,' she said as she walked across the office to the door. 'We'll be back in touch.'

'A *statement*? Hey, wait a minute!'

Kate closed the door on him.

'Son of a gun,' Taylor said, striding across the lobby to the bank of elevators. 'Let's hear it for routine police work.'

She was too elated to indulge in sarcasm. 'That page of numbers in Dory's van, Ed – have you figured out what they mean yet?'

'Nope. But I've sure figured out a few other things.'

An elevator arrived as Gabriel Koerner burst through his office door. '*Wait* a minute! I have nothing to do with this!'

Taylor gave him a cheery wave as the elevator doors closed. 'What about the numbers, Kate?'

'You'll see graphically in just a few minutes, Ed. Twenty minutes from now we'll learn by computer what Dory Quillin had to take a two hundred mile trip to find out.'

'I'm telling you the truth, Kate, I thought all the stuff about Dory's father was so much horseshit. I thought Dory made all of it up so she had an excuse for everything she felt like doing.'

'I can see how you could think that,' Kate conceded. The elevator doors opened at the main floor. 'But you were right about the one thing I never considered for a minute – that the Quillins were possibles.'

CHAPTER 15

Kate stared grimly at the computer printout from the
Network Communication System. The arrest record of
Roland James Quillin contained a single entry: Summerville,
Fresno County, California, July 7, 1964, violation of California Penal Code g288, seventeen counts. Charges dismissed
in Fresno, November 9, 1964. Penal Code g290 — registration
of a sex offender — would apply on conviction, Kate knew,
and she murmured this information to Taylor who whistled
softly, tunelessly as he examined the printout.

Kate shook her head, marveling at the ironic clue Dory
Quillin had left to point to her killer. Section numbers from
the California Penal Code — the provisions by which every
criminal suspect was arrested, tried, convicted.

Taylor admitted, 'I don't know section numbers off-hand
like you do, Kate.'

'I wouldn't think so.'

Eight years a homicide detective, he would be less likely
than most to know them. Patrol officers readily recognized a
good many of the hundreds of listings in the Penal Code; the
numbers were radioed to patrol cars to describe the nature
of a crime in progress or one newly committed. But detectives
tended to be most familiar with those in their particular area
of assigned investigation.

'Two-eighty-eight,' she said, 'lewd and lascivious acts
against children. Two-ninety, automatic registration of a sex
offender. I know those numbers well, Ed. From Juvenile.
They were familiar to Marietta Hall for the same reason —
she's been involved in so many cases with children. Even the

S Dory made was a clue – it was misshapen because she didn't know how to write the section symbol. Everything was right there, I knew it was there – I just didn't see it.'

'It would've come to you,' Taylor said confidently. 'But there was a third number, Kate.'

'Section two-eighty-five,' she replied. 'Incest. She applied that one to herself. Remember Neely Malone telling us Dory wanted to sue her father, and she was serious about it? We'll have to piece together where Dory went when she drove up to Summerville, but she had to ask questions to find those section numbers. Somehow she learned enough to end up at the courthouse in Fresno looking at the public record of that trial.'

'Maybe Roland Quillin still has relatives up there, Kate.'

'Possible,' Kate agreed. 'Koerner mentioned a Paula Jankowski – maybe Dory found her, too.'

'I bet she went to the library looking for newspaper accounts.'

'And to find out everything she could about these section numbers.'

'Kate, we got a lot to talk about now.'

'Let's get some food. I've been wanting bacon and eggs ever since – all day long.'

They sat in a booth at the coffee shop in the mini mall close to the station. Taylor added a Denver omelet onto Kate's order and then said, 'Quillin – he's enough to make me puke. The guy comes down here, right away marries sad sack Flora who probably figures she's lucky to get such a prize catch when she's not a spring chicken anymore, and then she presents him with just exactly what he's always dreamed of – a little girl he can do anything he wants to, whenever he feels like it.'

With effort Kate put images of Dory Quillin out of her mind, to concentrate on assessing the information at hand. 'Motive is the clearest thing we've got, Ed. Dory came back from her trip all primed, with all the goods on him.'

'Yeah. And you can bet your badge nobody down here knows he got busted up north, much less what for.'

Kate said soberly, 'Including his wife.'

'Especially her. And so Dory comes back from Summerville and he finds out he's in shit right up to his eyeballs. Dory all of a sudden has enough dynamite piled around him to blow the lid off his marriage, his livelihood, his whole fucking life not to mention his diseased dogshit pecker.'

Remembering Quillin's anxiety to keep secret any details about his disgraceful daughter, Kate added her own angry sarcasm, 'And besides, what would all the neighbors think?'

Then she had a new thought, and felt suddenly bleak. In the high excitement of adding this vital new piece to the puzzle, she had not stopped to look at the whole. She sipped her coffee, gathering her thoughts in a search for new perspective.

'Motive is really all we've got, Ed. No witnesses, no prints, no physical evidence other than Dory's list of numbers. Plus a wife who won't see what's going on around her and doesn't have to testify against her husband no matter what.'

Their food arrived; Kate looked at hers without appetite. Taylor dug into his omelet. 'Yeah,' he said, 'even so we still got damn good probable cause for an arrest.'

'Let's look at this realistically, okay? That arrest record of Quillin's is the only solid evidence we've got. Is it admissible? No. A jury would never even be allowed to *know* about the single arrest of a man who was never convicted. And what else have we got besides that? If we arrest Quillin I think we're looking at a case that'll end up a sure D.A. reject.'

Taylor's deflation was visible. He lowered a forkful of egg, stared down at it. Then he gestured with the loaded fork as he spoke. 'Hey, we still got one good chance, Kate. Maybe he'll cop to it.'

Not likely, she thought. No confession had been forthcoming when he was arrested up north.

'Let's pick up the son of a bitch,' Taylor said. 'Twist his pecker up behind his ass. See what he does.'

Reflecting on Taylor's words, feeling her hope and her appetite return, she picked up a half of her English muffin and nibbled at it; it was crisp and warm and buttery. She attacked her bacon and eggs.

A few minutes later, re-energized by the food, she said, 'I think we ought to talk to both the Quillins. Together.'

'You do?' Taylor looked up from demolishing his hash brown potatoes. 'Why her?'

'If she doesn't know what Dory found out up north, it might sink in more effectively if she hears it when we spring it on him. What'll she do when she finds out he not only molested Dory but killed her too?'

'You mean you want her there when we lay it on Quillin?' Taylor was incredulous. 'Jesus, I don't know about that, Kate. We could have all kinds of problems with that.'

'What've we got to lose? If she comes over to us, we could be looking at a case with whole new possibilities.'

'Having her there when we put it to him.' Taylor said the words as if chewing over them. 'You know, it could be real interesting, Kate.'

'It would put an enormous amount of pressure on both of them.'

'Yeah, but it's so off the wall — even if they *are* husband and wife. You sure we wouldn't be violating somebody's constitutional rights?'

Kate grinned. 'Why would we? Aren't a husband and wife one legal entity? A properly timed Miranda warning should take care of constitutional rights quite nicely.'

Taylor finished the last of his food and pushed his plate away. 'I have to tell you one thing, Kate. Nineteen years a cop, I never investigated or arrested anybody for messing around with little kids. I mean, I want to *kill* this creep.'

'I have my own strong feelings about him.' Kate looked at her watch. 'Let's get back. It's only three-thirty, we'll contact law enforcement in Summerville and get a clear picture of what's in Quillin's case file. Then we'll plan our very careful approach to Mr. and Mrs. Quillin.'

CHAPTER 16

Flora Quillin voiced her complaint mildly: 'I really did think we'd seen the last of you.'

Roland Quillin said nothing; but his grim face was faintly mottled.

As the Quillins stepped aside to permit Kate and Taylor entry, Kate deliberately led the way into the living room, and chose the armchair on a direct path to the door and with an unobstructed view of the sofa. She could smell food cooking: perhaps spaghetti sauce or chili. Taylor took the armchair to her right. The Quillins arrayed themselves on the sofa, just as they had the night Kate and Taylor had notified them of their daughter's death.

Kate made a disheartened assessment of Flora Quillin. If anything, the woman looked thinner, paler, more washed out and tired and insignificant than she had remembered. The cotton dress was of such a non-descript green that it seemed to fade into the chintz fabric of the sofa, while Flora Quillin's face blended into the faintly green walls of the room. By contrast, Roland Quillin in his bright yellow polo shirt and dark brown cotton pants projected burly strength and confidence. Yet it was Flora Quillin who would be the major factor in determining the outcome of this confrontation. . . .

'Mr. Quillin,' Kate said, 'we'll begin with questions for you. Would you please state your full name, date and place of birth.'

He examined her. She sat easily in the armchair under his scrutiny, her shoulders straight, knowing she was well prepared for him. Even Taylor, in the leaf-green jacket and white shirt and beige pants he had felicitously chosen to wear today, his lank, recently barbered blond hair neatly combed, appeared unusually substantial and businesslike.

'Roland James Quillin, August fourth, nineteen twenty-five, Fresno, California.' The answer was slow and patient, as if Quillin was exercising great reasonableness in choosing to humor her. 'May I ask why all this is necessary?'

'It's a necessary part of the inquiry into the death of your daughter,' she answered crisply, thinking that even with his baldness and the deep lines around his eyes, Quillin's barrel-chested build suggested strength and youthful vigor. 'Who would be your nearest living relatives?'

His dark blue eyes were coldly watchful. 'I have a brother, Fred Quillin. He lives in Hawaii.'

'How long has he lived there?'

'Years. I don't know, thirty, maybe. I don't see what –'

'Your parents are deceased?'

A nod.

'When?'

'My father in 'fifty-six, mother in 'fifty-nine.'

So no close Quillin relative had been living in Summerville in the summer of 1964. . . .

'Your occupation?'

'Tax accountant. Self-employed.' His gaze shifted from her face down to the notebook where she had swiftly jotted his responses, to the gray interoffice envelope beside her.

'When did you come to Los Angeles?'

There was a brief pause; then Quillin answered, 'Early sixties.'

'Dear,' Flora Quillin said, 'it was nineteen sixty-four.'

'Of course,' Quillin agreed, his face softening as he smiled at his wife. 'Being interrogated by the police is disturbing to me.'

I'm sure it is, Kate thought. I'm sure it's disturbingly familiar. She said to him, 'You were nearly forty years old in nineteen sixty-four. Why did you decide to leave Fresno?'

Quillin jerked his head up to glare at her. 'What does that have to do with anything?'

'Mr. Quillin,' she countered, 'why does the question bother you?'

Quillin crossed his thick arms; they seemed clotted with dark hair. 'This *situation* bothers me, Detective. Better opportunity, I came down here for better opportunity. Is there another reason why people move here?'

'I don't know.' Predictably, Quillin was stiffening his line of defense with increasing hostility. 'Is Mrs. Quillin your first wife?'

'Yes.' Quillin seemed to relax slightly with the question; he sat back and smiled at his wife. She gave him a faint smile in return, her hands tightly clasped in her lap.

'When were you married?'

Flora Quillin answered timorously, 'June fourth, nineteen sixty-five. Roland never remembers, every year I have to remind him.'

Deliberately, Kate ignored her. At this juncture she did not want input from Flora Quillin to add turbulence to the cross-currents between herself and Roland Quillin. 'When and where did you meet Mrs. Quillin?'

'At a church social,' he said easily. 'A month or two after I came down here.'

'Oh yes,' Flora Quillin affirmed. 'Roland wasted no time asking me to marry him.'

'And Dolores Quillin was born when?'

'May third, nineteen sixty-six.' Roland Quillin again smiled at his wife. 'Six pounds, ten ounces.'

Kate said quietly, 'And she died at the age of nineteen years.'

Roland Quillin looked down. 'God works in mysterious ways. . . .'

Flora Quillin fixed her eyes on the crucifix hanging on the wall to the left of Kate. 'The judgment of God can come at any hour – that's the first thing my Daddy ever taught me.' Her voice was tired, defeated. 'God's law has nothing to do with man's law.'

Pitying this woman and her bleak future, Kate could not help asking, 'Do you have relatives close by, Mrs. Quillin?'

'Why, no. My parents died young – in their forties, both of them. I have a sister, Frances. She's a teaching lay-missionary. She's been in Africa for years taking care of all those pathetic souls over there.'

130

Kate took a few moments to complete her notes and to reflect on the astuteness of Roland Quillin. He had found the perfect cover: a devoutly religious woman, one who would obey every tenet of her faith without question, including the biblical and priestly admonishments to women to accept the dominion of the male.

Kate turned over the page in her notebook, her signal to Taylor to take over the questioning, and Taylor said briskly, 'Ever had any difficulties with the law, Mr. Quillin?'

Quillin's expression did not change; he looked unblinkingly at Taylor. 'Meaning what?'

'Meaning have you ever had any difficulties with the law.'

Quillin said, 'I ran up against a surly traffic cop once.'

Very composed, Kate thought. It stands to reason – he's had years to prepare for this day.

Taylor said evenly, 'Have you ever been arrested or booked for a criminal offense?'

Quillin sat back, his legs braced, his arms crossed over his thick chest, and continued to stare at Taylor.

'Of course he hasn't,' Flora Quillin said with asperity.

Kate was careful not to glance at Taylor, and hoped he too had not given away the significance of Flora Quillin's confirmation that Quillin had indeed kept her in ignorance of his background.

'Mr. Quillin?' Taylor prompted. 'You've never been arrested or booked?'

'Can't say that I ever have,' Quillin replied.

'According to our records you were arrested in Summerville, California on July seventh, nineteen sixty-four.'

Kate was watching Flora Quillin; her pale blue eyes widened, then focused on the white-knuckled hands in her lap.

'*Why are you doing this!*' Quillin had bounced halfway out of the sofa to thunder the demand. 'What right, what *reason* do you have dredging that up! I was *acquitted!*'

Momentarily distracted by his dramatics, Kate swiftly returned her attention to Flora Quillin, who was staring, slack-jawed, at her husband.

'Acquitted?' Taylor repeated sarcastically. 'The case was

dismissed, Quillin, and only because your little victims didn't come forward to testify.'

'So what! What difference does it make! I was never convicted, you can't use that on me!'

'Victims? Little victims?' quavered Flora Quillin. 'Roland, what's all this about?'

'Nothing, Flora. Nothing, sweetheart, I promise you.'

Taylor moved forward in his chair, leaned toward Quillin. His voice was low, conversational: 'A jury was empaneled. There were two days of testimony from police officers and child psychologists –'

'You can't do this to me.' Quillin had lowered his voice, but the tone was malevolent. 'This is persecution, this is total invasion of privacy.'

'Your trial record is in a public file in the Fresno courthouse, Quillin. Now tell us what you were arrested for.'

'Nothing,' he roared, *'nothing!* They let me go, that *proves* it!'

Flora Quillin's entire face had gone slack. 'Roland, don't carry on so. Whatever this is, I'm sure it'll be all right.'

'Flora, I never meant to have you know about this. You didn't need to know. There was no sense in having you know.' Quillin's voice quivered with sincerity. 'I wanted to put all those terrible days behind me. Now these two have dredged all this up –'

'Quillin,' Taylor said harshly, 'you have the initial Q tattooed on the palm of your right hand at the base of the thumb.'

Quillin leaned forward and slammed his right hand on the coffee table, turned it over. The palm was calloused, but clear of any marks or scars.

'He had it surgically –' Flora Quillin broke off as her husband turned savagely on her.

'Don't give them any information,' he screamed.

'But Roland, when it's the truth –'

'Don't volunteer *anything!* Stay *out* of this, Flora!'

Kate watched Quillin's fury with satisfaction. If being married to a religious woman had its advantages, it also had its perils.

From the gray interoffice envelope she pulled her phone

notes and also the confirming teletype from Fresno. 'Marie Pankowitz,' she read, 'six years old, Clara Ross, seven years old, and Gena Grayson, also seven years old, stated to Summerville police officers that you took them over behind the girls' bathhouse in Kennedy Memorial Park and put your hand inside their clothing and fondled their genitals.'

'I didn't! I didn't do anything to anyone! You have no right to do this in front of my wife!'

'This is terrible.' Flora Quillin's voice was a shocked, husky whisper. 'Why are you saying these things to Roland? He couldn't do any of these terrible things.'

'Paula Jankowski,' Kate continued, 'seven years old, and Hilda Johnson, eight years old, and Jill Smythe, also eight years old, stated that you gave them an ice cream bar and then sat with each one of them on a park bench with a hand inside her panties while you had your other hand inside your pants.'

'You must stop this,' Flora Quillin whispered. Roland Quillin sat silently, his arms crossed, his face splotched red with rage.

'Jean Phillips, six years old, showed Summerville Police Detective Edwards the toilet cubicle where you took her in the girls' bathhouse, where you then took off her panties and performed an act of oral copulation.'

'*Stop this!*' Flora Quillin lunged as if to rip the papers from Kate's hands. Kate extended a swift, intervening hand, and just as suddenly Flora Quillin slumped back into the sofa. She whispered, 'Why are you doing this to my husband?'

'All seven of these little girls,' Kate continued, addressing Roland Quillin but with Flora Quillin clearly in her field of vision, 'accurately described your physical demensions. Six of the seven mentioned the tattoo on the palm of your right hand.'

Flora Quillin's thin features froze into immobility.

'Four of these children were set to testify,' Kate related from her notes. 'At the last minute the parents of all four refused to put them on the stand and have them confront you in court, to have them admit and describe in public exactly what you did to each of them.'

Kate slid her papers back into the gray envelope and said

conversationally, for Flora Quillin's ears, 'It's certainly not an uncommon occurrence. I know from my own experience as a police officer that cases of child molestation can be extremely difficult to prosecute. For the same reasons the case against you was dismissed.'

'It was lies,' Quillin said. Kate was startled by the calmness in his voice. 'The case was dismissed because it was a pack of lies – nothing more, nothing less.'

'Quillin,' Taylor said, 'where did you get that scar on your left cheekbone?'

Quillin said acidly, 'I walked into a door.'

'You walked out of that courtroom and into the fists of Paula Jankowski's father. Because he wasn't about to let you get off scot-free after molesting his seven-year-old daughter. The court bailiff took you to a hospital, you had stitches taken. And *that's* when you decided you'd better clear out of Summerville.'

'Roland,' Flora Quillin whispered.

'Sweetheart, I'm telling you none of this is true.' His voice was strong with conviction. 'You'd think these two officers of the law would know enough to presume a man's innocence if he hasn't been proven guilty, that's the way the law's supposed to work. A group of evil little children saw me in a park all those years ago, they made up a pack of lies about me. And *that's* why they wouldn't testify. Because it was all lies. As soon as these two officers of the so-called law –' He brushed a hand toward Kate and Taylor as if warding off insects, '– as soon as they leave our home, I'll tell you the whole nightmare. Now that they've forced me to.'

Kate watched Roland Quillin briefly place a hand over the clenched hands of his wife. As she had fully anticipated, there was no angle at which to approach him. He was not susceptible to any appeal to conscience or ethics – the conduct of his life had obviated that. By now he had undoubtedly traveled beyond any concept of conscience to the psychopathic stage of many criminals who rationalized any act, however monstrous. An uncooperative subject could occasionally be approached directly, with an appeal to logic and the subject's own self-interest; but Quillin surely realized that there were no bargaining chips here. In a capital crime of premeditated murder he had nothing to gain by cooperation.

Now that the preliminary stage of this interview was completed, a single path remained. If Roland Quillin was not fearful, surely Flora Quillin was. If he could not be reached through conscience, surely she could. If he lacked all moral character, surely she did not. If there was any hope at all for resolving this case, for compiling evidence enough to convict this man, that hope lay through her . . . This denying woman must somehow be made to understand exactly the kind of creature she had married.

'Mr. Quillin,' she said, 'we have substantial reasons to believe you're involved with your daughter's death, and for that reason we're taking you in for further questioning. I will now advise you of your rights.'

Flora Quillin made an inarticulate sound.

'That's *obscene*,' Quillin hissed.

'You have the right to remain silent,' Kate said evenly. 'Anything you say can and will be used against you in a court of law. You have the right to speak to an attorney, you have the right to have an attorney present. If you cannot afford an attorney, one will be provided without charge. Do you understand these rights?'

'I have *nothing* to hide.'

'Please answer the question. Do you understand these rights?'

'Certainly. Not that it matters – you've already violated my rights.'

'We have not. Do you wish to give up your right to remain silent?'

He looked at his wife, who was staring down at the hands in her lap. 'I told you, I have nothing to hide.'

'Do you wish to give up the right to speak to an attorney and have him or her present during questioning?'

'There's no reason I need an attorney.'

'Roland,' Flora Quillin whispered, 'we could call Charlie Howe –'

'I don't *want* an attorney,' Quillin said gratingly. 'I don't *need* one.'

Surely not one from his own parish, Kate thought wryly.

She turned her attention to Flora Quillin, who had yet to respond in any way Kate had hoped for. It was now imperative that she have further contact with this woman before Roland Quillin could exert his influence. 'Mrs. Quillin,' she said softly, trying to keep from her tone any element of entreaty, 'you're free to come down to the station if you wish.'

'Flora, you stay right here,' Roland Quillin ordered, then added more gently, 'I don't want you there, sweetheart. I'll get all this straightened out, I'll be right back home.'

'Of course I'm coming, Roland.' The voice was whispery and distant. 'I have to be there.'

'Will you be able to arrange your own transportation, ma'am?' Taylor inquired courteously. 'You can't accompany us, I'm very sorry but it's regulations.'

'Of course. . . .'

'Flora, listen to me. I don't *want* you there. You stay *right here.*'

But Flora Quillin rose and drifted soundlessly over the hardwood floor to the dining room table where she picked up her purse; she disappeared into the back of the house, presumably to a door leading to the garage.

Taylor stood and pulled out his handcuffs. 'On your feet, Mr. Solid Citizen. Hands behind your back – just like you did it last time.'

Taylor sat at the head of the table in the interrogation room, Kate and Roland Quillin on either side of the blond wood table with its formica top. Unknown to Roland Quillin, the room's tape recorder had been switched on. Kate had finished filling out form 5.10, the lengthy Investigator's Final Report with its many blocks of information on the details of Roland Quillin's everyday life, past and present. Flora Quillin, in a bird-like fluster of distress that she could not accompany her husband into this room, had accepted Kate's assurances that Kate would soon talk to her, and was waiting down in another interrogation room.

The best chance with Roland Quillin, Kate knew, was to goad him into mistakes by making him angry and defensive. From the gray interoffice envelope she drew out the plastic-protected original of Dory Quillin's Penal Code numbers and said coldly, 'Recognize this, Quillin?'

He gave it a single glance, then focused his dark blue eyes on her. 'No. What does it have to do with me?'

'Your daughter made this. You don't recognize even one of these numbers?'

He looked at it again, more searchingly. 'Doesn't mean a thing. What are they?'

She did not reply, and slid the evidence back into the envelope, knowing her action would unsettle him. It was possible that he in fact did not recognize the numbers; and by no means would she reveal the significance of this prime piece of evidence.

'Quillin,' she said, 'account for your whereabouts on Sunday June sixteenth at approximately six o'clock in the evening.'

'I was home,' he retorted. 'Right in my own house. Taking an afternoon nap.'

Taylor snorted, and Quillin's eyes narrowed. 'My wife will support that,' Quillin said acidly.

Kate said, 'You've already stated that you concealed your arrest record. Why didn't you tell your wife?'

'I *told* you, I was never convicted, I had every right to put all that behind me.'

'Quillin, we're not idiots.' Kate raised her voice. 'You didn't tell her because you knew you could safely indulge your filthy sexual appetite for children whenever you wanted – with your own daughter.'

'That's –' Quillin broke off as Taylor leaned toward him, into his face.

'When did you find out your daughter took a trip to Summerville?'

Roland Quillin raised his eyebrows, raised his hands as well. 'I don't know a thing about that.'

Again Taylor snorted, and Kate shook her head to convey her own skepticism.

Taylor said, 'Your daughter found out all about your dirty little life, Quillin. We know it and you know it. She went up there to get the whole dirty story of what she found out down here.'

'*How* did she find out?' he demanded.

Deciding that a few details would increase the pressure on him, Kate said, 'She met somebody who remembered what you did in the summer of 'sixty-four, Quillin. And we've found him too. Your daughter checked court records in Fresno and discovered what she had for a father – something that usually crawls out of a sewer.'

Glaring at her, his hands forming into fists on the table's formica top, Quillin opened his mouth to speak, closed it.

'She learned all about the saintly father who threw her out of her own home,' Taylor said contemptuously. 'The saintly father who molested helpless little girls, the younger the better. The saintly father who got busted and came an eyelash close to doing time in the slammer. So much for keeping dirty little secrets, Quillin.'

Roland Quillin stared at Taylor, his face contorted with fury.

'She contacted you when she returned from Summerville,' Kate said. 'So come out with it, Quillin. When did the contact take place?'

'It didn't.' Quillin uttered the words around gritted teeth.

Taylor snapped, 'How often did you molest your little daughter, Quillin?'

'Never,' he snarled. 'If you talked to that shrink of hers, you know all about how she accused somebody else of the same thing. That *proves* she was a liar.'

Taylor said sarcastically, 'Funny coincidence how your daughter and seven other little girls up in Summerville all turned out to be liars.'

Kate said, 'She lied to protect you. She lied and ruined another man's life to warn you away – because she couldn't stand the vile things you did to her every day of her young life. Because she didn't know the kind of scum she had for a father.'

Taylor said, 'She lied to protect your scummy worthless life, Quillin.'

'No,' Quillin returned, 'she just flat-out lied.'

Kate said, 'She ran away when she was fourteen to get away from you and the filthy things you did to her, Quillin.'

'You're not putting any of that on me, sister. I had nothing to do with what she did to herself. I had nothing to do with her becoming a lesbian and a hooker. And you won't get anything out of my wife,' Quillin spat, 'because she doesn't believe that either.'

Kate said, 'We *know* you committed acts of molestation and oral copulation on your daughter. We *know* you did it every day from the time she was five years old.'

'Then prove it. What you're saying is stupid and worthless. Because you have no proof.'

Kate said, 'The night we made our death notification, you and your wife stated that your daughter still called home occasionally. So by your own admission you still had contact with her. She came back down here from Summerville and confronted you, didn't she?'

'I never saw her. I never talked to her.'

'You knew she went up there, what she found out.' Taylor's heavy voice seemed to bounce off the room's acoustical tile. 'You knew she'd use it to prove what you did to her. She'd tell her mother, tell everybody, maybe even take you to court. She'd mess up your entire life. So you went over to the Nightwood Bar and you sat in your car in that parking lot and you waited for her. And then you killed her.'

He did not answer.

Taylor said contemptuously, 'Cat got your tongue, Quillin.'

Quillin crossed his arms.

'You molested your daughter from the time she was five years old. And then you killed her. Didn't you, Quillin?'

Quillin said slowly, precisely, 'You've got all the answers you'll ever get from me. I didn't kill anyone. I didn't do anything to Dolores. You can rake over my arrest record till you're blind. Make all the wild accusations you want. You can't make anything stick.'

Kate inclined her head to Taylor, and rose.

Taylor got up, leaned over close to Quillin. 'We're just starting on you, asshole. When we're through, *you'll* be through, you slimy piece of dogshit.'

'Take a flying fuck,' Quillin said.

Outside the interrogation room, Kate studied Roland Quillin through the one-way window. He sat relaxed at the table, an arm along the back of the chair beside him, an ankle crossed over a knee.

'The man's impervious, Ed,' Kate said. 'If there's such a thing as reincarnation, he used to be a cockroach.'

'Yeah. Or maybe a rattlesnake with no rattles. Like you figured, the wife's really all we've got and sad sack Flora flipped her switch to off years ago.'

'I think it might be better if I talk to her solo,' Kate said.

'Yeah, okay.' Taylor was watching Quillin. 'The son of a bitch,' he muttered. 'I gotta go to the john. And barf.'

'I might be right behind you. Don't forget to handcuff him to his chair.'

'Yeah. Handcuffs look real natural on that bastard.'

Flora Quillin's pale eyes looked glassy. She answered Kate's question in a disconnected voice: 'Why, I guess Roland was home all last Sunday.'

Kate looked across the table at her in consternation. This woman who would not see what she chose not to see, was she in the process of a full mental retreat from the meaning of everything she had heard?

'Last Saturday and Sunday, did your daughter call your husband? Did she come over to the house?'

Flora Quillin shook her head.

'Mrs. Quillin, listen to me. We *know* your husband committed acts of molestation and oral copulation on your daughter on a virtually daily basis from the time she was five years old.'

Flora Quillin dropped her hands into her lap; she sat slumped in the metal chair and stared down at her hands.

'Yet she loved him, loved you both enough that she ruined an innocent man's life because it was the only way she knew to warn your husband away from her. She did come to you and tell you that, Mrs. Quillin. She did tell you, didn't she?'

'What?'

In dismay Kate repeated her statements and added, 'She *did* tell you your husband was molesting her, isn't that right?'

'Oh. Well, yes, it was some time after the business with the teacher. She did say she made that up to protect Roland. I didn't believe her.'

Flora Quillin's voice was so astonishingly calm, so matter-of-fact that Kate stared at her helplessly. 'Do you believe it now?'

Flora Quillin looked at her then, and the pale blue eyes were opaque. 'I need to talk to Roland about that, you see.'

'No, Mrs. Quillin, I don't see.' Kate raised her voice, wanting to force the mind of this retreating woman back into this room. 'What I see is a man who chose not to tell his wife about his past because he knew he could safely indulge his sexual appetites whenever he wished – with the daughter you gave him.'

There was no response.

Kate said, 'Then he threw your daughter out of her own home, discarded her because she was inconvenient and making trouble, and she was no longer interesting to him for sex anyway. And then she learned the whole truth about her father – that he not only violated her, but committed the same despicable acts on other little girls.'

Wishing she could physically pound on Flora Quillin to make her listen, Kate said, 'Your daughter found out about him only four days before she was killed, Mrs. Quillin. Imagine how she must have felt. Imagine her despair in making that two hundred mile drive. Imagine her reading through that court record of her father's violation of other children. Imagine her feelings when she learned that her father – your husband – willfully and deliberately destroyed her childhood. Took away her innocence for his own vile satisfactions. Destroyed any possibility for her to have a relationship with you, her own mother. And then, Mrs. Quillin, he completed his destruction of your daughter by taking her life.'

Flora Quillin did not change expression; her eyes were focused on the hands in her lap. Had she heard any of this?

'Mrs. Quillin,' Kate pleaded, 'you know what I'm telling you is true. You know it in your heart.'

There was no response.

With a sigh she did not try to conceal, Kate took the page of penal code numbers again from the gray envelope. What did she have to lose by showing them to Flora Quillin?

Without help from her they had no case whatsoever. 'Look at this, Mrs. Quillin.'

Obediently, Flora Quillin lifted her head, stared at the plastic-covered page.

'This was your daughter's last act before her death. They're penal code numbers. The numbers she discovered up there in Fresno, the ones that were used to arrest and book your husband.'

'She wrote a note,' Flora Quillin said in her matter-of-fact voice. She pointed to the page of lined yellow note pad paper. 'On paper like that. She left it in the mailbox.'

Finally – finally she had broken through. Kate pursued her eagerly. 'When? Mrs. Quillin what did the note say? Tell me what it said.'

'I forget,' she whispered, and the pale blue gaze drifted away from Kate.

Kate wanted to go over the table at her. 'Mrs. Quillin, please look at me.' The gaze swung obediently back to Kate, searched her face uncertainly.

'The note said she had proof of her father's crimes against her. Isn't that what it said?'

'I forget.' The pale blue eyes were again opaque.

'Do you still have the piece of paper?'

'No. . . . It being just more of her craziness, I threw it away.'

'Did you show it to your husband?'

Flora Quillin squeezed her eyes shut and shook her head, the small lips pursed into invisibility. It was not clear, even when Kate repeated the question, whether she was responding to the question or refusing to answer.

'Mrs. Quillin,' Kate said, 'think carefully. Do you want to be an accessory to murder? The crime of murder is against man's law *and* against God's law.'

Flora Quillin said, 'I've let you speak, to have done with all this. Are you through with your questions for Roland? Can we leave now? I don't feel a bit well.'

Kate closed her eyes, sagged in her chair. The woman, she remembered, had recently undergone cancer surgery. 'Mrs. Quillin,' she said tiredly, 'just once in your life stop deluding yourself. Seven little girls identified him in Summerville. How many more little girls were there who never came forward at all? Do you have any idea what your husband does whenever he leaves your house? How many other innocent little girls' lives he's damaged? He may be your husband, but do you want to harbor a killer? A killer who murdered your own daughter?'

'It's not true,' Flora Quillin whispered, her eyes still shut.

Kate lost control. 'It *is* true,' she shouted. 'Look into your *heart*, Mrs. Quillin. What your daughter found out, what she wrote on that paper she left in your mailbox, was *true*. The man you married was never the man you thought he was. He was a . . .' She searched for more words to describe this vampire of a man who drained the innocence from young children, but at the sight of Flora Quillin's closed eyes and face, she conceded defeat.

She took out one of her cards, wrote her home phone number on the back. 'Call me, Mrs. Quillin. Either here or at home. Any hour of the day or night. Your own life could be in danger. We have every reason to believe your husband has killed once. If he could kill his own daughter –'

'Please,' she whispered. 'Just let us go now. I'm really too tired.'

Kate nodded. She said bitterly. 'You and your husband are free to go.'

At the door of the interrogation room Flora Quillin paused to transfer the straps of her purse from her hand to her thin shoulder. Kate could see that the palms of each hand contained four crescent-shaped red wounds.

CHAPTER 17

After Roland Quillin had been released, Kate sat glumly with Taylor in the interrogation room.

'It was a good plan,' Taylor told her consolingly. 'Laying it out to the Quillins was the only shot we had, Kate.'

'That may be,' she said, 'but I have to tell you I'm having second thoughts. About Flora Quillin specifically. I warned her, Ed — but still, if she's the only viable witness against him —'

'I'm not about to lose any sleep. Quillin figured we'd never link him to Dory, but if he does anything to sad sack Flora we got him by the short hairs and he knows it.'

'He might skip.'

Taylor shrugged. 'Where to? He's been playing Mr. Solid Citizen for too many years. If half the info he gave us on that five-ten is right, we got a dozen ways to sunset to track him. Besides, the guy's no kid anymore to be running all over the countryside. Kate, we got nothing on him, he knows it. He seemed pretty sure about his wife, too — and he knows her a hell of a lot better than we do. I say let's do what we can. Ship his description around to all our people. You can bet he's been on the prowl since Dory left. What's the statute of limitations on two-eighty-eight?'

'I need to check but I think six years,' Kate answered, nodding.

'So, any victims in all that time who described a husky guy with a scar on his left cheekbone, Mr. Solid Citizen gets to spend his time standing in lineups. Who knows? Maybe we'll skin his ass yet.'

'I haven't given up totally on his wife,' Kate said, remembering the fingernail marks cut into Flora Quillin's palms. 'Maybe something of what happened here got through.'

'Yeah. Maybe. Never underestimate a woman, right?' But Taylor looked dubious. 'I figure if we don't hear in the next day or two, we'll never get a thing outta sad sack Flora.'

Kate nodded again. She herself hoped to hear from Flora Quillin tonight. She sat up in her chair, raised her arms, stretched her back and neck muscles. 'God. I'm tired, Ed. Really bushed.'

'Let's go home, partner,' Taylor said. 'It's been one damn long hell of a day.'

At her desk Kate took out the card Andrea had given her, picked up the phone. That she remain home tonight was imperative in case Flora Quillin called; but perhaps Andrea would come over.

Sorry, I can't come to the phone right now. If you'll leave your number after the beep, I'll get back to you just as soon as I can. Thanks.

Sorely disappointed, feeling even more tired, Kate glanced at her watch: seven-twenty. Probably Andrea was still out on a real estate appointment. She would leave a message. . . .

Then she remembered the pleading voice last night, the ex-lover named Bev whom Andrea had avoided for two months by intercepting her calls on this heartlessly automatic answering machine. Repelled by the thought of leaving a message on the same machine, she hung up. She would call from her apartment; Andrea would surely be home by then. . . .

Kate changed into jeans and a T-shirt, poured herself some scotch, slid a TV dinner into the microwave, put Sarah Vaughan on the tape player, and tried Andrea again. And tried her again at eight-thirty.

Unsettled and depressed, she sat in her easy chair with her feet up, her head back and her eyes closed, listening to the caramel voice of Sarah Vaughan vibrate in the stillness of the room, feeling too tired to move when the tape finally clicked off.

Of course Andrea had a job that kept her confined and busy. Who better to understand that than she herself? All those times she'd spent long hours away from Anne with only a hurried phone call in explanation, and sometimes not even that . . . And Andrea could not call her – she did not have Kate's phone number. Kate had not remembered to give it to her, nor, for that matter, had Andrea asked . . .

Stop this, she told herself. Stop being ridiculous.

She had only to be patient. She was in the same position as Ellen O'Neil had been in with her more than a year ago. What Ellen had wanted she could not give – surely not then, not five months after Anne's death. Andrea was only two months away from breaking up her own long-term relationship, she was still in pain . . . The fact that she and Andrea had gone to bed together had been an aberrant event based on separate needs, just as that night with Ellen had been . . . The best and only chance for this new relationship was to give it time to grow, all the time it needed. To allow Andrea to finish processing through her breakup with the woman named Bev.

Still, it seemed that Andrea should be there tonight to take her call. Because they *had* gone to bed together – and what they had shared was not meaningless. Andrea had said she would be there. *Of course*, she had replied to Kate's question would she be there. Her lengthening absence seemed to take away more and more from the significance of their night.

Kate looked broodingly across her dimly lit apartment, and finally pushed her thoughts away, exchanging them for anxiety over Flora Quillin. She became impatient with those thoughts as well. Nothing, there was absolutely nothing she could do about either Flora Quillin or Andrea Ross.

The phone rang. Kate came out of her light doze and leaped for it, glancing at the clock: nine exactly.

'Detective Delafield? This is Flora Quillin.'

'Yes,' Kate said eagerly. 'Are you all right, Mrs. Quillin?'

'All right? Well . . . yes, I would say so. . . .'

As Flora Quillin's voice drifted off, Kate strained to listen; she could hear the rumble of an engine – perhaps a bus or a truck — then fainter traffic sounds; the indefinable conglomerate noise of a city street. Flora Quillin was at a pay phone.

'Mrs. Quillin, are you sure you're all right? Where are you?'

'The reason I called,' Flora Quillin announced in a voice that was suddenly clear and distinct, 'I want to know, where is the body of my daughter?'

'At USC Medical Center,' Kate answered, nonplussed. 'Since it hasn't been claimed, the coroner's office —'

There was the sudden blaring of a horn.

'Oh dear, that's Roland,' Flora Quillin exclaimed, and hung up.

Kate replaced the receiver, staring at it. What on earth was happening? Where were the Quillins, and why? And what was going on in Flora Quillin's head?

Perhaps the Quillins were en route to claim their daughter's body — but why call from a pay phone to find out where Dory's body was? Flora Quillin had not seemed troubled or agitated in the least; she had not seemed in any kind of danger. But something felt odd, something felt very *wrong* about that phone call.

Helplessly, Kate picked up the new *Time* from the coffee table. She switched on the television set and settled back into her easy chair. Then she focused on her other anxiety. She would wait, she decided, till nine-thirty to try Andrea again. She flipped open the magazine.

At exactly nine-thirty she poured herself another scotch and dialed Andrea's number.

'Hello!' It was a soft, cheerful, female voice. Not Andrea's voice.

Kate cleared her throat. 'I'm calling for Andrea, is she there?'

'Hang on.'

A hand was placed over the receiver but Kate could hear the raised voice, the muffled words: 'Phone for you, want to take it in there?' There was a pause, then the cheery voice said, 'I didn't ask Andy.'

Kate now recognized the voice.

A receiver was picked up, apparently from 'in there,' and the other receiver was hung up.

'Hello, this is Andrea.'

'It's Kate.' She sat in her armchair staring numbly at the television screen, at a weatherman in front of a cloud-covered map of the western states. 'I'm sorry to disturb you, I see you have . . . someone with you.'

'Yes,' Andrea said quietly. 'I didn't think things would move quite this fast, but they have. Bev is here.'

'Yes,' Kate said. 'I recognized her from the answering machine last night.'

'You're a very good detective.'

Kate heard the smile in Andrea's voice. 'At times I can be a terribly poor detective,' she replied.

The reason for Andrea's formality this morning was so very transparent now – why had it not been equally clear to her then? All the evidence had been there. Andrea had said: *I was never unfaithful to Bev the whole time we were together. . . .*

'Kate, we've known each other such a very short time,' Andrea said. 'Not long enough for any hurt to come to either of us – am I right about that?'

'Right,' Kate said, forcing positiveness into her tone, closing her eyes.

After the way Bev was about my surgery she could never have been the first woman in my bed. . . .

Maybe not the first woman, but surely the second.

For the first time in my life I needed validation as a woman. And I had to have it from you. Not from Bev. . . .

She had received that validation. And it was all she wanted from Kate. It was clear why the answering machine had been on this evening, and where the 'in there' was that Andrea had taken this call.

Kate said, 'I wish you only the best. I think you have better things to do right now than talk to me.'

'Kate . . . Goodnight, Kate.' The voice was soft, sincere: 'I hope we can be friends. Can we still be friends?'

'Of course. Good night, Andrea.'

Hands in her back pockets, Kate slowly paced her living room. She remembered the oddness of Andrea's tone this morning when she had answered *Of course* to Kate's question about being home tonight. She now recognized the tone:

perfunctory. She had used the same tone herself in replying to Andrea's question about remaining friends.

There was no way they would be friends. She would not flagellate herself by being around a woman she desired and had been in the process of falling in love with, knowing that that woman belonged irrevocably to another. And Andrea would not wish to be around the woman with whom she had slept – regardless of her justification for the act – to remind her of her unfaithfulness to the woman she truly loved.

Kate turned off the television. She could hear the faint whoosh of traffic on Montana Avenue; a car alarm ululated in the distance. The apartment seemed large, dark, echoingly empty.

She tossed *Time* back onto the coffee table, pulled the *Law Enforcement Legal Reporter* out of the magazine rack. Tucking the publication under her arm she walked into the kitchen and poured her drink down the drain. She did not feel like drinking. Or reading. Or watching television. Or thinking. Especially thinking. She would go to bed and try to read her periodical and perhaps she would fall asleep doing that.

She sat down on the side of her bed and picked up the framed photo from her night table and held it in both hands, gazing at the light-haired, smiling young woman in jeans and a red checkered shirt leaning up against a weathered gray fence, gray ocean in the background – the photo had been taken on a trip to Oregon.

'Why did you have to leave me?' she whispered. 'Ever since you left, everything has just gone straight to hell.'

CHAPTER 18

Awakened by music from her clock radio, Kate unwillingly sat up and swung her legs over the side of the bed. Remembering the events of the day and night before, she added the weight of depression onto the heavy tiredness in her limbs.

She trudged into the kitchen and poured coffee from the automatic coffee maker, pausing to sip from the steaming mug before taking it with her into the bathroom. Twenty-five minutes later, her preparations for work complete, she sat in her living room and picked at a plate of scrambled eggs and toast, trying to distract herself with the *CBS Morning News* and the *Los Angeles Times*.

She folded the paper and dropped it onto the carpet, clicked off the TV with the remote control. No point in avoiding this, she thought. She might as well look at both her failures square on and get on with it.

Although her time with Andrea Ross could hardly be rated a failure — not when intrusion into an exclusive love had never been the remotest possibility, not even a might-have-been.

But the Dory Quillin case — was that a might-have-been? True, there had been a failure of corroborating events: witnesses and physical evidence, precious little of the coincidence and plain luck that sometimes descended like a blessing on a homicide investigation. But there was also the nagging feeling that something else still lay within her field of vision, something she had not quite seen, something that might have helped place Roland Quillin behind bars where he belonged.

Even under ideal conditions, she thought venomously, his

crime would not qualify him for the electric chair. Not in California where the prerequisite for the death penalty was murder of a particularly heinous nature, the always problematic 'special circumstances.' Wishing such punishment on Roland Quillin was irrational and vindictive, she conceded; monster that he was, the death penalty still seemed a basic waste of creatures like him. They should instead suffer the more useful fate of assignment for scientific study and experiment, for whatever could be gleaned from a malign cannibal subspecies which had lost the moral right to be treated as anything other than laboratory fodder. Especially a subspecies which preyed on children. . . .

Kate rose, pulled her notebook from her shoulder bag, leafed through the pages of notes, a cryptic recording of this failed investigation. And it was a failure of the worst kind – for they had pinpointed Dory Quillin's killer only to allow him to continue to roam the streets, only to put him on guard so that he would perpetrate his acts with greater vigilance in the future.

She thought about Marietta Hall whose determination to make headway in the sewage of crimes against children had foundered, collapsing into exhaustion and bitter recognition of futility. She had promised to remain in touch with this woman, to keep her informed. What could she say to her? Kate looked slowly over her notes of the conversation with the psychologist, many of the phrases evoking clear and powerful memory of that interview.

FQ CONVINCED DQ LIED
DQ HOPED FOR ATTEN TO WARN RQ OFF
ABUSE STOPS WHEN PERP SEES THREAT TO SELF
KD: DID DQ TELL FQ?
MH: NO GREATER RISK. MANY MOTHERS DENY. COMPLETE DENY AT ANY COST

Marietta Hall's words echoed in Kate's mind: '. . . a very common response from many mothers is denial. And I mean *complete* denial. Denial at any cost. Denial of evidence right in front of their eyes. . . .'

Denial at any cost. . . .

Stunned into immobility by the new design she saw for her facets of information, Kate sat perfectly still for some time, her mind tumbling, reassembling facts. Finally she got up and moved trance-like to the phone. It rang under her hand.

'Kate? This is Lieutenant Rodriguez.'

'Yes, sir,' she answered in full alertness at the clipped tones of Lieutenant Manuel Rodriguez, the watch commander. She had grown to like him for his business-like briskness; he indulged in the amenities of politeness and small talk only in the absence of pressing police business.

'The damnedest thing, Kate. A car fire right next to the station. The parking lot, that mall over there. One fatality. Olds Omega, 'eighty-two, we checked DMV, it's from that case you and Ed —'

'The Quillin case,' she confirmed, scarcely able to get the dry-throated words out. 'I remember the make and model from a five-ten I filled out just yesterday.'

She was trying to assimilate what he had said, needing to get whatever other information he had, desperate to get off the phone and be on her way to the scene. Flora Quillin. Flora Quillin had called her last night from a pay phone . . . She had been with Roland Quillin. . . .

One fatality . . . *One.*

'A license plate blew off when the gas tank went up or we'd have the devil's own time figuring out this much this soon. We got a body over there so charred we can't make any ID.'

'I'm on my way this minute. Sir, will you call Ed?'

'He's next on my list.'

'Thank you.' Kate slammed down the phone, grabbed her shoulder bag and jacket, ran for the door.

Not having the Plymouth with its red emergency light, Kate wove her Nova aggressively through the early morning rush hour traffic, leaving a blaring trail of furious drivers all along the familiar path through Santa Monica and West L.A. She roared past the brick Wilshire Division station, always a bastion of solidity amid the drab landscape of Venice Boulevard, past the Broadway Savings and Loan on the corner, and screeched into the parking lot of the mall, pulling to a stop in front of Zody's.

The blackened, steaming hulk of a car sat in the side

parking lot of the Savings and Loan, perhaps a hundred feet from the station house. Four black-and-whites, two fire trucks, and a fire department official vehicle surrounded it. Thick clusters of silent spectators crowded the sidewalk, held back by a half dozen officers and a yellow tape barricade.

Kate picked her way carefully over the asphalt parking lot which was stained and puddled with chemicals from the extinguishing of the car. Her nostrils quivered and recoiled from the acrid stench. She remembered a trip along the coast she and Anne had taken in the aftermath of a forest fire, the noxious fumes that had reached them from the charred and smoking corpses of dead trees and animals. . . .

She nodded to Hansen, who impassively returned her nod; then she circled the wreckage. Taking measured breaths against the stench, she peered into the car, at the black-red remains of a figure behind the steering wheel, its hands drawn up and hooked like claws. She knew the posture was typical of a fourth degree burn victim, the claw-like hands the result of contraction of cooked and charred muscles. She resisted memory, forcing her mind away from her very personal knowledge of burn trauma on the human body.

Hansen came up to her, clipboard in hand. 'The Quillin tragedy continues,' he intoned. 'Pretty obvious it's suicide, from the look of it.'

'You're wrong,' she said shortly. 'Tell me what you've got, Fred.'

He looked at her, then obediently recited, 'Pearson turned it in at six-fifty-eight. Saw the car going up like a torch as he was rolling out of the station. Couldn't get near it, said it was an inferno. These guys –' Hansen motioned with his clipboard to the fire truck and the official car, '– they were here in less than two minutes. Chief Scarborough –' Again Hansen motioned with his clipboard, toward the official car and the black man in a Battalion Chief's hat who was writing on his own clipboard, '– he says the inside of the car was soaked in gas, the victim as well. That, plus the gas tank – not much wonder it went up like a bomb.'

A yellow Honda Civic pulled into the parking lot next to Kate's car; Taylor climbed out, yanked his blue plaid jacket out of the back seat, and shrugged into it as he walked over, splashing heedlessly through the chemical puddles. He clapped Hansen on the shoulder, glanced at the corpse in the steaming wreckage, shook his head dolefully at Kate. 'Should've listened to you, partner,' he said. 'The son of a bitch went and did it to sad sack Flora.'

'No he didn't, Ed. It's Roland Quillin in that car.'

Taylor stared at her; and Hansen lowered his clipboard and peered intently into the charred wreckage as if to verify her identification.

'Okay, Kate,' Taylor said calmly. 'So how do you figure it's him?'

Kate ignored him. 'Fred, did Pearson see anyone leaving the scene?'

'No, Kate. He checked around thoroughly, so did the rest of us when we got here. But there were a lot of spectators, really fast.'

And Flora Quillin, Kate thought, scanning the crowd outside the tape barrier, could fade into the pavement, much less a background of spectators.

'Fred,' she said, 'send a car to the Quillin house. It's –' She reached into her bag for her notebook and read him the address. 'She's fiftyish, no more than five-two, maybe a hundred pounds, dyed blonde hair. It's not likely she'll be there, but we still have to check it out.'

'Right, Kate. I take it she's a suspect?'

'Right.'

Hansen hurried off.

'Kate,' Taylor said patiently, 'I feel like I'm on a whole different planet from you. I don't figure what you're figuring here at all.'

'It only came to me this morning. I was just about to call you when Rodriguez got me. Dammit, Ed, it was classic misdirection. I was so intent on one solution I never even looked at anything else. Flora Quillin heard every single word we said yesterday. She didn't respond because she realized what I should have seen too – that if she came forward, Roland Quillin would walk away a free man. Because Roland Quillin didn't kill Dory. Flora Quillin did.'

Again he stared at her. 'Kate, I know I'm not the brightest guy –'

'I'm the stupid one.' She bit off the words. 'It was all there, I should have seen it. Flora Quillin had exactly the same motive as Roland Quillin – to prevent Dory from blowing her whole life apart. In a different way she had as much to lose as her husband. Marietta Hall gave us the first clue about Flora – that some women deny child abuse by their husbands at any cost.' She raised her voice in emphasis: '*At any cost.* We had corroboration from Neely Malone. Flora Quillin herself showed us that she wouldn't see what she didn't want to see – that she'd rather abandon her own daughter than look at the kind of man she married and the kind of lie she was living.'

The odor from the burned car again assailed Kate; she moved further away. 'Flora made only one mistake yesterday – telling me about that note Dory left in their mailbox. My guess is, Dory wrote to both parents about what she'd found out in Summerville, threatening to sue and spread scandal and make very major trouble. Flora Quillin found the note. My next guess is, she never showed it to Roland Quillin. She told me she destroyed it and I think she probably did.'

'So you figure Flora came over to the Nightwood Bar, not Roland.' Taylor's tone was skeptical; he scratched his bald spot and then layered the hair back over it.

Kate nodded. 'To try and reason Dory out of what Flora thought was just her latest craziness. My theory is that Dory said she had incontestible proof about her father. And Flora being Flora, she wouldn't see or hear that proof. She saw only that Dory had come up with a terrible new way to bring more grief and maybe even financial ruin to their lives. So it was Flora Quillin who picked up that bat and killed her.'

'And yesterday Flora finally sees how wrong she's been.' Taylor's tone had not lost any of its skepticism. 'So she decides to knock off Roland because she knows we can't touch him for any of the things he did to Dory or anybody else.'

'Yes, Ed. You see? Yesterday we forced her to look at the truth. She had no choice but to own up to it, and by the standards of her religion was well.'

'Yeah?' Taylor gestured to the car. 'So why didn't sad sack

Flora torch herself along with her husband? How come we don't have two bodies in there?'

She indulged herself in a sardonic response. 'Because murder is justifiable, but suicide is against her religion.' Then she said impatiently, 'She may still do it for all we know. That's why we have to get moving and find her.'

Taylor scratched his head again, sighed. 'It's so goddam crazy it *sounds* like it could be right. But there's one big major flaw in your theory, Kate. How'd sad sack Flora manage that all by herself?' Again he gestured to the blackened car, the darkly crimson corpse. 'How'd little Flora knock off big husky Roland who's twice her size?'

'I don't know,' she admitted. 'The fire department people say the car and the victim were doused with gas. Somehow between last night and seven o'clock this morning Flora managed to get him helpless and keep him helpless till forty minutes ago.'

He said sarcastically, 'And she very thoughtfully brought him right here next to the station so we wouldn't be inconvenienced. I don't buy it, Kate. You're dead wrong on this one. You were right the first time about Flora being in danger. It's Flora in that car, and Roland put her here and he's on his way outta town laughing his head off.'

'Ed —'

'Hear me out, Kate. *Look* at this car, for chrissakes. Even if Flora's holding a *gun* on him, is he gonna sit there and let her pour gas all over him and then strike a match? Anybody'd rather take a bullet in the head than *burn*, for chrissakes.'

'So maybe she shot him first,' Kate retorted. 'Look, right now she's got unfinished business. She called me from a pay phone last night wanting to know where Dory's body was. I think that's where she is.'

Taylor jabbed at the burned car. 'And *I* think *that's* where she is.'

She turned, walked toward her Nova. They were wasting too much time with all this arguing. They would drop their personal cars off at the station, take the Plymouth . . .

Taylor was hurrying to keep up with her. 'Dammit, Kate, the only thing Flora could shoot is a popgun. The recoil from anything else'd knock her into the middle of last week. Sad sack Flora doesn't have it in her to shoot somebody, much less turn her husband into barbequed ribs.'

Kate did not reply.

'She wouldn't even *try* something like this, Kate. I mean, you know better than I do women don't do this shit.'

We don't very often, Kate thought, opening her car door. But we're capable.

'Ed, I don't have a clue how Flora pulled this off. But I do know one thing – she'll talk to us now. And we've got to pick her up fast in case she decides to do something to herself. Let's get the coroner and the technicians out here, it's all we can do here anyway.'

'Okay, okay,' Taylor grumbled. 'I still think we oughtta be checking airports for Roland Quillin.'

'And I think Flora Quillin's at USC Medical Center. Because I can't see her going there last night with Roland Quillin. We'll check with the hospital on the way and stay in contact with the car that's checking the Quillin house just in case.'

'How'd she get out of here without a car?' His sweeping hand took in the wide boulevard. 'She catch a bus? How'd she get *anywhere* for chrissakes without us seeing her leave?'

'I don't know that either,' Kate said, sliding into her car.

'If you're right about any of this,' Taylor said, yanking open the door of his Honda, 'I'm an idiot and you're Sherlock Holmes.'

You're definitely an idiot, she thought sourly, slamming the door of her car, but as far as this case is concerned, I'm Inspector Clouseau.

CHAPTER 19

'Seeing is believing,' Taylor muttered from beside Kate.

Flora Quillin, dressed in black, a small cloth purse in one hand, a black book in the other, was strolling the corridor outside the Coroner's Office, her head down. Kate guessed that the severe dress with its long sleeves and square cut neck was probably the one she wore to funerals or formal functions at her church.

'But Jesus, who'd believe sad sack Flora . . .' Taylor trailed off as Flora Quillin, seeing them, walked briskly down the corridor toward them.

'I thought this was the best place to wait,' she said, 'not having a car and all. And knowing you'd figure all this out,' she added to Kate.

'It took me long enough,' Kate answered, seeing that the book was a missal. Flora Quillin's face was pale, but seemed calm, almost serene. She smelled faintly of gasoline.

'I'm grateful it wasn't any sooner. I needed to do everything I did.'

'Mrs. Quillin, we're placing you under arrest.' Kate reached to Flora Quillin and delicately but firmly took the purse from her.

'Yes, of course.'

Taylor said, 'I'm sorry ma'am, but we'll need to handcuff you.' He had palmed his cuffs in his big hand as if embarrassed.

Nodding, awkwardly clutching her missal in both hands, Flora Quillin held out her wrists; they seemed scrawny as birds' legs.

'I'm sorry ma'am, it'll have to be behind your back. It's regulations.'

'Oh. Well, that's fine.' She handed the missal to Kate, turned her back to Taylor, and placed her wrists together. 'A nice young man allowed me to see Dolores,' she said as Taylor snapped on the cuffs. 'Of course her body is only the shell for her soul, but I thought being here with her might bring my prayers more directly to her. Since I'll soon be joining Roland,' she added in an untroubled voice, 'in suffering the punishments of eternal damnation.'

Kate and Taylor moved down the corridor, Flora Quillin between them. They entered the lobby, Flora Quillin jingling the handcuffs with the motion of her walk. An older couple halted in mid-stride to stare. Kate thought: If you only knew. This tiny, innocuous-looking woman has bashed her daughter's head in and turned her husband into a charred corpse.

Flora Quillin leaned toward her to whisper, 'You do very good work, Detective Delafield. I've always known that the best people on this earth are the ones who take on the most terrible jobs.'

At Wilshire Division, in the interrogation room where Roland Quillin had been questioned the day before, Kate and Taylor sat with Flora Quillin.

Kate recited the Miranda warning and said, 'Do you understand these rights, Mrs. Quillin?'

'Yes, my dear,' she answered in a clear, calm voice. 'And please do call me Flora.'

'Flora,' Kate obediently repeated, 'do you choose to give up your right to silence?'

'Yes, my dear.'

'Do you choose to give up your right to an attorney?'

'Yes indeed.'

'At this point, would you tell us in your own words about the deaths of your daughter Dolores and your husband Roland.'

'Well, Dolores called the house –'

'When was this?'

'Last Saturday morning, it was early, Roland was out

watering the roses and so he didn't know at all what was said –'

'But you did tell your husband that Dory – I'm sorry, Dolores had called?'

'No, I never did, not till last night. And go ahead and call her Dory. If that was what her friends called her, it must be the name she liked most. I used to call her that when she was little, you know, before . . .' Flora sighed; her eyes welled with tears. Her pale hands, spider-webbed with tiny blue veins, slid over the formica table top, translucent fingertips touching, then stroking the leather spine of her missal.

'So I talked to her. She was upset, she was saying terrible things about Roland. I turned my head off like I always did, like I learned to do years back . . .' She looked at Kate in anguish. 'I guess you know by now I was the cause of all this trouble – me not listening to the things she said.'

You weren't the cause. Your husband was. But Kate returned her gaze with a sympathetic murmur and a receptive nod, knowing it was imperative that she not detract from the guilt which was at the root of this full confession.

'Well, she got so hysterical I finally hung up. She called right back and I told her . . .' Flora's voice faltered. 'I told her to go away and leave us alone. I told her that so many times before, so many times when she called . . . Oh heavenly Maker of us all. . . .'

Kate reached into her shoulder bag, fished out a purse size packet of tissues.

'Thank you, my dear. Well, later that day I went out to get the mail – it doesn't come till early afternoon – and there was this note from Dolores . . . from Dory,' she amended. 'She'd come over and I guess just put it in the box.'

She dabbed at her eyes with a tissue, blew her nose. 'Well, she said in the note that she wanted to talk to me, and she was going over to Father Jamison and show him some kind of proof Roland was a child molester. Well, I guess you know I saw it to be more craziness from her, except this time she'd come up with some new kind of scheme to hurt Roland's reputation and the way he made his living. That's how I looked at it, you see.'

Again Flora dabbed at her eyes. 'Well, after thinking on it

the rest of Saturday and most of Sunday, I decided I should talk to her –'

'Flora,' Taylor interrupted, 'your husband – he was aware of none of this?'

'No, and the reason was, well, I didn't want him upset, and last Sunday was Father's Day, you know. Remember I mentioned it to you?'

'Yes, Flora, I do remember,' Taylor said softly.

'It seemed most particularly cruel, it being Father's Day – so I didn't mention this new trouble. And see, what you don't know is, the time was coming that I'd have to tell him how my health was troublesome again, you see. . . .'

Was she referring to her cancer surgery? Kate glanced at Taylor, signaling with a brief shake of her head that they should not interrupt Flora Quillin at this point to ask.

'I left the house about four or so, Roland being asleep on the sofa. I wrote him a note I was down visiting Alice, she's three doors away. Well, after driving all that way to that place Dolores – Dory was staying, she wasn't out there in her van. I couldn't bring myself to go in there, into that . . . that bar to see when she'd be back, but I stopped one of those women –'

'Who?' asked Kate, frowning at Taylor. Why hadn't this woman – whoever she was – stepped forward to mention this? 'Can you describe her?'

'Well, she had this very short black hair, she was masculine-looking, you know. I could never understand about Dol – about Dory being one of them, she wasn't a bit like that . . . Anyway, this woman was wearing denim pants, with a vest made of it too, with embroidered circles with crosses on them in the front. In a little while she came back out, I guess she'd just gone in for cigarettes, she said Dory was at a ballpark, she'd be back around five-thirty. Then she climbed in her pickup truck. . . .'

Coincidence. Luck and timing. If that woman had remained at the bar, this homicide would have been solved immediately. . . .

'So I decided I'd wait. And about quarter to six I guess it was – just when I had to get home and fix Roland's dinner –

here she finally came, driving up the hill in that awful looking van of hers. And I got out of the car –'

Kate thought: So I was wrong about when Dory made those numbers. It was before she went to the park. Somebody probably interrupted her, wanting her to play baseball . . . and she went off and simply left the pen uncapped. . . .

'Well, I guess she saw me. She climbed out, she was wearing that white baseball suit . . . So I came up to her and I said just as quiet as you please, "Dolores, it's Father's Day."

'Well, she began to laugh. This terrible laugh like she'd gone crazy . . . The truth be told, I was all of a sudden afraid of her. So then she flung open the side of the van and plain ordered me in and I said I didn't want to, but she went inside and I didn't have the choice but to follow her, you see. Then she picked up that pad and showed me those numbers you showed me yesterday and told me things about Roland, about the trip she took, the same things you told me yesterday, she shook that pad at me – you see?'

Kate nodded. 'Yes, Flora,' she added for the sake of the tape recorder.

'I shook my finger right back at her, I told her she was making more things up, and she yelled at me then, how she'd go about making everybody in the world believe her, even take Roland to court, and then I'd have to believe her too.'

She stared pleadingly at Kate, the whites of her watery pale blue eyes bloodshot. 'I had surgery you know, for the cancer in my womb. I couldn't see before why I suffered all the pain there, why God was making me suffer so, but now I understand. And I understand why He's put the new cancer in my liver.'

Kate looked at Taylor, wondering if her face had the same blankness as his as he too absorbed this information and its meaning. She gathered her wits and asked, 'Your husband, he didn't know about . . . the new cancer?'

Flora shook her head. 'I hadn't wanted to tell him, not till I had to. You see, the doctors told me there was nothing to be done about it this time. It was all part of the reason I was so frantic over Dory – I knew I wouldn't be here much longer to do for him. And I told her all that, I told her about the cancer. And she began to cry, she said Roland had done it to me too, he'd killed everything around him including her and me both. And she was going to get him, she was going to kill him right back for all he'd done . . . And that's when I said, you stop that foolishness or I'll tan your hide just like when you were a bad little girl. And she all of a sudden started that laughing again.'

Flora rubbed her eyes; her shoulders heaved in either a sigh or a sob; Kate could not tell which. 'The truth be told, I thought the devil himself had taken possession of her. I'd always suspected deep inside maybe it was the devil that had possession of her all along, maybe that was why she did the things she did. She said she was going right to Father Jamison, she jumped out of that van and I picked up the bat and came right after her, I had to make her stop . . . She turned around to say something else and then I remember this look on her face like she couldn't believe what she was seeing. . . .'

Flora Quillin seized Kate's wrists; her grip was fierce, the hands hot and dry. 'Next thing I remember . . . it was the most terrible sound, it was sickening, like one time in the car when I ran over a bitty squirrel and I could hear its little bones crack . . . and Dory was on the ground looking at me and trying to get up, and all I saw was, I'd driven the devil out of her, you see?' She was squeezing, pulling on Kate's wrists. 'I thought *God* was the one who'd directed my hand. That's what I actually *believed*, you see?'

Kate was sick with pity, sick with the memory of Dory Quillin's disbelieving face, the silver-blue eyes staring up in supplication, in bewilderment.

'*You see?*'

'I see,' Kate managed to acknowledge her.

Releasing Kate, Flora put her face in her hands, then quickly sat erect and nodded vigorously. 'But now I know all this time, all these years, it was the devil in *me*, acting through me and Roland. It was the devil in possession of us both.'

Kate glanced at Taylor; he shrugged almost imperceptibly, rolled his eyes.

'I went home. And there was Roland still asleep, never knowing I was gone, nor what I'd done. There I was back in my own house, believing in my soul God's judgment had been done through me, it was the hand and will of God in my last days on this earth that directed me to destroy Dory to protect Roland. . . .'

She looked at Kate and whispered, 'Before I go on, could I possibly have some water?'

Kate nodded approval to Taylor, who rose. 'Be right back,' he said.

Kate waited until he returned with a styrofoam cup and handed it to Flora, and waited again while Flora dabbed her reddened eyes dry of tears and swallowed several sips of water.

'Flora,' Kate said, 'would you tell us now what happened from the time you and your husband left here yesterday?'

'Yes indeed,' Flora said. Her voice had strengthened and was suddenly calm; her eyes were opaque. She turned her palms up and Kate saw the scabbed-over crescent-shaped wounds she had noticed yesterday; she remembered seeing that same opaqueness in those eyes when she had described to Flora Quillin the meaning of her husband's crimes.

'Roland talked to me on the way home, he asked me questions, but I can't rightly tell you what about or anything I said . . . because I was too busy thinking how it was I should go about doing what needed to be done. I knew it was all my fault you see, he was my mistake to fix, because there was nothing you people could ever do to him for what he did to Dory and God knows how many other of those little girls. . . .'

She closed her hands, began to dig her nails into the stigmata-like wounds. Kate grasped the hands, gently straightened the hot dry fingers. Flora withdrew her hands from Kate's, placed them over the missal.

'Roland was never interested in me after Dory was born, you see, after we found out I couldn't be pregnant again. And all this time I'd felt guilty about it and plain grateful that he still wanted me with him when I couldn't give him more babies . . . Come to think on it now, I do remember one thing he said after we got hime. He said the man had the dominion over his family, and the man had the right to run his family as he saw fit, and it was nobody's right under any law to question that. And if I was unhappy about anything I should think on how it would be to fend for myself, without him. I do remember Roland said that. It didn't matter much what he said because I knew what I was going to do, you see.'

Flora's opaque eyes stared off into space for so long that Taylor finally prompted her, 'So then what did you do, Flora?'

'Oh. Well, I figured I couldn't take a knife or an ax to him, he's too strong, I couldn't chance him stopping me, you see. So I fixed his dinner, I had homemade chili simmering in the electric kettle from before you both came to see us. I waited till he was in the bathroom and then I sneaked out to the garage, that's where we keep the rat poison, we've always got rats trying to get in there. Then I served up his bowl of chili and I stirred in some of the rat poison, you see.'

She was looking expectantly at Kate, and so Kate replied, 'Yes, Flora.' She resisted the urge to rub gooseflesh from her arms.

'But I didn't know how much to use, you see, and I didn't want him noticing it, or the chili tasting so bad he wouldn't eat it. So I sprinkled maybe a teaspoon in, and put a tiny bit in his coffee, and then after dinner when he wanted another bourbon besides the one he'd had before dinner, I added a little bit to that, too, you see.'

Again she was looking intently at Kate. 'I see,' Kate responded.

'It was right after he finished the bourbon that he got sick. He knew right away what I'd done. You poisoned me, he says. No I didn't, I told him, wanting to give it more time to work, it's the chili, Roland, it doesn't agree with you. By then he's staggering around the room holding his stomach, he grabs the phone and dials the nine-one-one emergency number, you know, and then he finds out the phone doesn't work. I'd thought about that, you see, and taken scissors to the phone cord, the end coming out of the wall so's he wouldn't notice. I was afraid then he'd go to the Morrisons next door even though we've never got along with them, but I'd planned for that, too. I'd taken the ax in from the garage when I got the rat poison and hid it under the sofa, just in case.'

Flora sipped her water. Kate marveled at the steadiness of

the hands, the evenness of the voice relating these details of calculated murder.

'But he didn't. He went staggering out the side door and into the garage, so I knew he was going to drive himself. Well, that wasn't any good either, so I quick got the ax and ran after him. But he got to the garage and that was all the farther he could go. He got real sick, vomiting all over the side of the car until he was so weak he couldn't lift his head. And I took the car keys away. And that's when he started to say please, please to me.

'He was still throwing up the poison and I could see it maybe wasn't going to kill him right away or maybe not at all, but he was too sick from it to move and I knew I had him and it was done. Now I could think about Dory and all the things he'd done to destroy the lovely child she was and turn me against her, and it didn't seem enough to just take the ax to him . . .

'So I helped him get in the car saying I was going to drive him to the hospital. But after that I got right out of the car and went about my business and all the time he's vomiting and saying please please, you see?'

'I see,' Kate said in chilled fascination.

'Roland kept a five gallon can of gas in the garage, he put it there during that gas shortage time. I always told him it was dangerous and he should get it out of there, but he ignored me about that just like he did most everything. Well, I unscrewed the cap and got one of my saucepans out of the kitchen and tipped all that gas out, pan after pan of it, and soaked him with it, his hair and his clothes and most particularly between his legs, and then I poured the rest of it inside the car. He was still vomiting, he had the diarrhea too, and he's saying please please because he knew I was going to burn him up, you see.' She paused, obviously waiting for Kate to respond.

'I see,' Kate whispered.

'But then I saw how crazy it was to do it there, it would take the whole house, maybe the neighbors too, and that didn't seem right. And besides, I still needed to find my daughter's body, speak to her. I knew he couldn't get out of the garage or even out of the car, so I went in the house and cleaned up and changed into this dress, it was more appropriate, you see, for what I was going to do next. And of course I got my prayer book. I decided I'd drive him down here, you see. I'd noticed this big shopping center when Roland and I were here, it seemed a good place to come, to make it easier on you folks to take care of what you needed to do after I was finished with him.'

Kate exchanged a glance with Taylor, remembering his contention that Roland Quillin had left his wife's body on their doorstep as a ghoulish joke. Taylor returned her glance with a now-I've-heard-everything roll of his eyes.

'Him not knowing what I'd planned, I think he figured I was taking him to get help. He even looked glad to see your police station. So I drove in here and parked over there.' She gestured, as if to a place in the room. 'It was quiet and empty, like I figured it would be. And that's when I went to the pay phone there and called you to find out where Dory was.'

'I believe it was about nine o'clock,' Kate offered quietly, for the benefit of the tape recording.

'I guess it might have been. But when I left the car to call you, Roland managed to crawl over and push on the horn, weak as he was. So I went back and shoved his hand away, and of course he was too weak to do anything to stop me. But still, he scared me. I didn't know but what he might think of something else to try. So I told him I was going to burn him up right then and there, but then I saw I'd come away with no matches. Neither Roland nor I smoke, you see.'

'I —' Kate cleared her throat, fighting back an almost irresistible urge to laugh hysterically. 'I see.'

'So I got down in the back of the car and took my brassiere off. I used it to tie his hands to the steering wheel, you see.'

Flora smoothed her hands down the front of her dress, over her concave chest, and said wonderingly, 'I've never allowed my own husband to see me like this, and here I am sitting in a police station and I'm not wearing my underwear.'

'You look just fine,' Taylor rumbled.

Flora jerked away from him in dismay, her eyes widening, and Kate said soothingly, 'It's all right, Flora, there's no problem at all, you're perfectly all right.' Why, she thought wrathfully, did Taylor never have the sense to know when he should keep his damn mouth shut? She said softly, 'Tell me what happened then, Flora. What did you do next?'

Flora looked at her, her pale blue eyes softening. 'Oh. Well, so then I went into the drugstore that was a little ways down the shopping center,' she said firmly, 'and I asked the first man I saw smoking, a nice young fellow in spite of such an awful habit, it was one habit Dory never had at least, I asked him please could he spare a book of matches, and he was very obliging.'

Kate thought: If he could ever know. . . .

'God forgive me for my anger, for breaking so many of His commandments, I decided to wait as long as I could about Roland. I'd take out that book of matches every little while and act like now I was going to burn him up, just so I could hear him say please please, just so I could ask him each time, did Dory say that to him whenever he did those things to her all those many times and all those many years, just so I could keep telling him he was going to feel what hellfire was like pretty soon and then for all the rest of eternity.' Staring at Kate out of wide, stricken eyes, Flora whispered, 'The worst thing is, I'll soon be there with him.'

Kate could not help trying to give some measure of comfort: 'If God is supposed to forgive . . .'

'Not this,' she whispered. 'I'll pray to Him, but how can He forgive all of this? So then, when the cars started to come by, the people going to work, I knew it was time. I got myself a soda pop can off the parking lot and weighted it down with keys from Roland's key ring and change from his pocket, and whatever change I had in my purse. And then I found an advertising flyer and stuffed it in, I made it into a fuse.'

She told Kate conversationally, 'I had a grease fire in my kitchen once, so I knew all about how fast fires go up and I had to be well away from there or I'd go up right along with the car and Roland. So then I waited till there was no traffic along the street there, and I lighted the paper in the can and stood as far back as I could, knowing I had to get it through the window of the car, you see.' She paused, looking at Kate.

'I see,' Kate uttered.

'Roland is looking at me, you see, and saying please please please, and I say, this is for all the innocent little lives you've soiled and fouled, go to the devil where you belong, this is for my daughter. And I threw it, and Roland turned into flame right in front of my eyes.'

Kate closed her own eyes for a moment, trying to dispel the image. When she was sure of her voice she said, 'And then what happened, Flora?'

'Why, I right away walked into your police station here.'

'Jesus,' Taylor expelled.

'Please, young man,' Flora chastised him.

'I got here none too soon,' she continued, 'I saw one of your squad cars coming around the corner. Then a nice young officer was very obliging about helping me get a cab.'

Taylor moaned.

Who, Kate thought ruefully, would ever question or suspect a tiny woman dressed in black and carrying a missal?

Taylor said in a kindly tone, 'And that's all the story, Flora?'

'Except I felt I should do away with myself along with Roland, but I needed to see my daughter and there needed to be somebody to explain all this, and besides, my passing on is going to happen soon enough anyway.'

'We'll make you as comfortable as we can, Flora,' Kate promised.

'I don't deserve comfort. My trials on this earth will be nothing compared to the hereafter.'

'Flora, we're going to type up a statement for you to sign,' Kate explained, 'and we'll have to take care of a few other things. We'll put you in a holding cell for the time being and then transport you to the Sybil Brand facility for women.'

'That's just fine,' Flora said serenely. 'As long as I have my prayer book. I used to read Dory a children's Bible when she was little,' she said, her eyes distant, 'but she like to drove me crazy with all the questions . . . She was such a smart little thing, always asking why. Like one time I turned on the light in her room and she had to know right then where the light came from and how it came on and why the light bulb was the funny shape it was and a million other questions . . . There couldn't have been another little girl like her, ever. So pretty with that blonde hair, I used to tell her God plucked the down from angel wings and made it into her hair . . .'

Flora shook her head. 'She was such a wild, free little thing, even when she was real small. I could never get that out of her. The truth be told, I never even dreamed about the things she thought she could do when she grew up. It just wasn't how women were in my time, you see. Why, I remember . . .' She trailed off, smiling, lost in reverie.

'Tell me something,' she suddenly said to Kate. 'You're out in the world so much more than I am . . . I know she was giving herself to men and it was a terrible thing to do, and it was for money. But that woman she took up with for so long, why ever would she do such a thing?' She sagged in her chair. 'I suppose Roland drove her to that, too.'

Kate said carefully, 'We talked to the woman Dory lived with. It was obvious she loved Dory very much. I believe she helped Dory a great deal with the pain of what her father did to her. I think your daughter loved other women because it was her nature. A lot of people are just simply that way, Flora.'

Flora looked suddenly sick and exhausted. 'I can't accept that, you see, what you say. It's against all the laws of God.' Flora closed her hands into fists, and winced; she opened them and looked at the palms as if aware for the first time of the wounds.

Kate pointed to the book that lay between herself and Flora. 'There may be answers in there. But we live very narrow lives if we think all answers are in one book. All the answers will *never* be in one book.'

Flora shook her head. She picked up her missal. 'I've got to believe what's in this book is His will on earth, and so I can't accept what you tell me.'

Kate rose, knowing that further argument was useless, and feeling the death of Dory Quillin as an even more leaden weight.

Kate led Flora Quillin from the room to put her in a holding cell. Then she returned to the interrogation room.

Taylor sat with his feet up on an adjacent chair, drumming his pen on the table.

'When we take her to Sybil Brand,' Kate said, 'we'd better have a suicide watch put on her.'

'Yeah,' Taylor said. 'Gotta do it. All that trouble seems real dumb when her cancer's gonna take her, and real fast.'

Kate nodded. 'She'll never see a courtroom. So, Ed, sad sack Flora finally stopped being a sad sack.'

'Yep. Now she's fruitcake Flora. Jesus, Kate. Marie and me, we go to church once in a while but – Christ, you know something? They ought to put a statement on the Bible just like they put on cigarettes – like, the contents of this book may freeze-dry your brains.'

CHAPTER 20

At ten-fifteen p.m. on this Thursday the Nightwood Bar was bright with light and filled with animated conversation; *Hill Street Blues* was on the television set and the melancholy contralto of Anne Murray came softly from the jukebox. There were perhaps twenty-five women present, including those Kate had met only an hour after the death of Dory Quillin. Except for Andrea Ross.

Kate nodded to Maggie; then to Patton who had turned around on her bar stool to greet her with a mock salute; then to Audie and Raney who were smiling at her from a table where they were playing Scrabble; then to other women whose faces she had come to recognize in the four days since Dory Quillin's death.

Kate went up to the bar, leaning across it to tell Maggie, 'I have an announcement. Could you make it a little quieter in here?'

Maggie studied Kate for only a moment, then reached for a switch under the bar, turned the volume on the jukebox down to inaudibility, accomplished the same for the TV over the bar.

Conversation ceased; faces turned to Kate and Maggie.

Kate raised her voice to take in the room: 'I wanted to let you know we've had a break in the homicide of Dory Quillin. We've made an arrest.'

A rising wave-like murmur was silenced by shushing sounds from Maggie. Kate braced herself for the reaction to what she would say next.

172

'We've arrested Flora Quillin. Dory's mother. We have a full confession.'

Amid silence that rang in her ears, Kate looked into gaping faces.

'Save us all,' uttered a gray-haired woman Kate did not know. 'Her *mother*?'

Patton leaped off her bar stool. 'You arrested her *mother*?'

'Yes,' Kate said soberly. 'She –'

'Her *mother*?' cried Audie from her table. 'How could her *mother* –' Audie broke off, as if the next words were unutterable.

Kate looked at the stunned faces of Tora and Ash, of Kendall and Roz – of all the women in the Nightwood Bar. How to explain the Quillin family, the dark enormity of this tragedy? Yet how to spare these lesbian women, many of whom had suffered grievous pain inflicted by their own families? How to prevent the black shadow of Dory Quillin's death from further staining this bar, these women?

'She went crazy,' Kate said.

'It's the only explanation,' Maggie declared from behind her, to Kate's gratitude.

Raney said, 'I thought sure you'd tell us it was those creeps from the other night. You *sure* about this?'

'Yes,' Kate replied. 'She's confessed to this crime as well as the homicide of her husband, who burned to death early this morning.'

'Fucking shit,' Patton exclaimed amid other gasps of amazement and horror from all around the bar.

Patton shoved her hands in the pockets of her jeans, hooking her thumbs through the belt loops, and rocked back and forth on her jogging shoes. 'You're right, the woman's gotta be totally out of her tree. So – what else can you tell us?'

'What else do you need to know?' Kate returned, not unkindly. 'You saw Dory out there in the parking lot, you saw what was done to her. What is it you want to know?'

'*More*, dammit. More than just telling us a crazy woman took Dory's life away.' Then Patton shrugged and muttered, 'Something to make us feel better.'

'Dory's mother is dying of liver cancer,' Kate said. 'Her doctor tells us she has six weeks to live, at the outside.'

'That doesn't do it. Not for me. That doesn't make me feel one goddam bit better.'

'Nor me,' Kate said. 'Dory's death is a senseless, useless waste.' She did not attempt to keep the vehemence, the bitterness from her voice.

'Dory tried to talk to me about her parents,' Patton said mournfully. 'I wouldn't listen. I told her to just let the hell go of them.'

'Patton, I told her that too,' Maggie said, 'and we were both right. I'm telling all of you,' she addressed the roomful of women in a firm voice, 'we can't choose our parents, but we sure as hell can choose how we feel about them. Why should we love anybody who doesn't accept or respect us? Besides,' Maggie said, her voice lowering to its usual soft tones, 'we have the power in us to make our own families.'

'This is some of my family,' Tora said, gesturing with both hands to the roomful of women. She added with a faint smile, 'I like big families.'

Kendall said, 'Roz and me, we go to the Metropolitan Community Church. You talk about a terrific big family . . .'

'Bookstores,' said a tall dark woman Kate did not know. 'I found a whole gay *world* through all the stuff I found in feminist bookstores.'

The room became warm again with the sound of animated conversation, a few tentative beginnings of laughter. With attention diverted from her, Kate said to Maggie, 'Do you have a few minutes?' She pointed to a table toward the unoccupied front of the bar.

'Yeah. Let me get us some coffee. Roz, take over, will you?' Maggie reached under the bar to her switches and piped Diana Ross into the room.

A few moments later, the smoke from a Pall Mall drifting up past her white thatch of hair, an untouched mug of coffee in front of her, Maggie sat with her hooded eyes fixed on Kate.

Kate smiled. 'I'm being x-rayed.'

'There's a lot more to this business with Dory than you've let on.'

Kate replied with a shrug; she would not lie to this woman. 'Maybe you'll talk about it one of these days,' Maggie said. 'Maybe.'

'You're very good at what you do, Kate.'

Kate shook her head. 'I often feel inadequate, Maggie. So much effort to accomplish what seems to make very little difference. What you do here seems a lot more important than what I do.'

'Believe me, you make a difference. We're both of us strong women. I think we have to share our strength however we can. I think both of us do that.' Maggie shrugged, flicked ash from her cigarette. 'I could never be a cop. I don't think you'd be real thrilled being a bartender.'

'Maybe not.' Kate looked at her with renewed interest. She had been curious about Maggie since their first meeting. In the coming days, as she spent occasional time in the Nightwood Bar, perhaps she would learn more about this enigmatic woman. She said with a smile, 'Strong woman, I have a favor to ask.'

'Sure.'

'Dory's body is still at USC Medical Center. Other than her mother, there's no one, just two relatives in different parts of the globe. I'll tell you this, Maggie – Flora Quillin understands the dimension of her crimes. So much so that she's rapidly moving into catatonia. She won't be capable of anything at all very soon.'

'That woman shouldn't have one thing to do with burying Dory,' Maggie said sharply, stubbing out her cigarette. 'Dory should be buried by her real family, her own people.'

'That's what I think, too,' Kate said. 'Would you take charge? I'll see about pulling the necessary strings on my end. Neely Malone told me Dory would have wanted cremation, with her ashes scattered at sea.'

'I'd have guessed that.' Maggie rubbed her jaw. 'I was at a cremation service just last year that was done pretty well, everything simple and nice. I think I can get it done the same way and for not too much money. Neely doesn't have a dime, you know. But we've saved up about three hundred for AIDS Project L.A., we can use part of that, I'll put in some of my own. I'm sure we can raise –'

'Don't do any of that.' Kate pulled her checkbook out of her shoulder bag.

Maggie picked up the check Kate had made out. 'You don't have to do this, Kate.'

'Yes I do,' Kate answered.

'I'll get on it first thing tomorrow.' She gestured to the women in the bar. 'I'm sure they'll want to attend. They damn well better,' she added. She tapped a finger on the check. 'I don't think I'll need this much.' She grinned at Kate. 'If I don't, how about the rest of it going into the AIDS fund?'

Kate nodded. 'Sure.'

Maggie folded the check, slid it into her shirt pocket. 'You off duty now? Can the house buy you a drink?'

'I'm off duty and I'd like a double scotch on the rocks, but the house can't buy it for me.'

'You're such a hardnose,' Maggie grumbled, getting up. 'Come on over to the bar.'

Maggie set Kate's scotch down in front of her. 'By the way, I haven't seen Miss Deep Freeze in a couple of days.'

It took Kate a moment to remember that this was Maggie's appellation for Andrea Ross.

'Seems real strange,' Maggie said, 'after seeing her in here for hours every single day the last two weeks. I've been in this business a long time, that woman was sure as hell looking for something.'

'Maybe she found it.' Kate picked up her drink. 'Here's to Miss Deep Freeze,' she said.

As Maggie went off to wait on a woman at the end of the bar, Kate relaxed into her tiredness, listening contentedly to all the female sounds around her.

'So,' Maggie said, coming back to her. She raised an arm toward the banner hanging above the mirror: ALIVE WITH PRIDE IN '85. 'You coming to the Gay Pride parade Sunday?'

Kate shook her head. 'It's too well covered by the media. And patrolled by the Sheriff's Department. I know some of those people – it's just too risky.'

Maggie leaned across the bar and gestured to the back of the room, toward the parking lot. 'Two nights ago you put your life on the line out there. You could get killed tomorrow doing your job. And you tell me you can't go to a Gay Pride parade. Doesn't that strike you as just a little weird?'

'Yes,' Kate answered, 'it does. But –'

Patton came up to the bar. She pointed an accusing finger at Kate's drink and held her nose. 'Yechhh,' she said.

Then she swept off her yacht cap and bowed low to Kate. 'Your officerness, Raney and Audie have challenged the two of us to a game of Scrabble. What do you say we go over there and kick ass?'

Kate looked over to where the two women sat smiling at her. 'You're on,' she said to Patton.

EPILOGUE

Streams of pedestrian traffic filled the sidewalks on both sides of Westbourne Avenue, young men and women who looked, Kate thought, less than half her age. She had found a parking place with difficulty, drifting her Nova up and down the streets south of Santa Monica Boulevard from San Vicente to La Cienega before discovering a niche to tuck the car into. The weather forecast had called for a smog-free day in the low eighties, and she had donned shorts and a favorite T-shirt; but the unfiltered sunshine defeated both sunglasses and a visor. Squinting, her eyes watering, she walked up the street toward Santa Monica Boulevard.

A much wider swath of humanity flowed up and down the Boulevard, feeding into the north side of its median strip which was lined on both sides with spectators, many of them packed up against storefronts on the far side of the street. A mounted brown-clad Deputy Sheriff trotted slowly by. Kate looked up into the smiling face of the middle-aged deputy who looked vaguely familiar to her. His eyes did not register her; he was intent on scanning the crowd ahead.

Down the street opposite the Tropicana Motel was a small section of bleachers, and Kate headed toward it, thinking she might stand in its shade. The bleacher was nearly filled; but she inquired of the plump young man in a Hawaiian shirt who guarded its stairway, 'Is this all reserved seating?'

His white teeth were brilliant in his bearded face. 'For you I can arrange a seat for a mere six dollars. To fight AIDS.'

She paid him, thanked him, accepted a green ticket stub, and climbed the stairs and over feet until she reached the end of the third row. Her companions in the bleacher were of various ages, most of them wearing shorts and tank tops or T-shirts, many of the men wearing no top at all. A number of styrofoam coolers were stashed under the slab-board seats. From everywhere around her came laughter and shouts, a high-pitched buzz of anticipation.

'Welcome, have a beer, join the bleacher party,' said the blue-eyed blond beside her, offering a can of Michelob. He wore snow-shite shorts and rope sandals, his hairless chest pink in the sun; Kate thought him one of the handsomest men she had ever seen.

'I'd love to,' she said smiling, 'but beer makes me warm and I'm already hot.'

He leaned down, fished in his cooler, drew out a Coke dripping with frost. 'So here you are, dear.'

'You're wonderful,' she said, accepting the Coke, snapping open its top.

'You are too,' he answered, and turned back to his companion, a bearded older man who, Kate decided, was even more handsome than the blond.

She drank in thirsty appreciation from her ice-cold Coke and looked out across the street. The young men and women, some sprawled at the curbside in lawn chairs, seemed incredibly handsome, graceful, confident, happy. There were constant shouts of greeting to new arrivals, people leaping to seize each other in spinning hugs. Exhilarated by the scene, Kate watched with the proud, indulgent pleasure of a parent, occasionally wincing as she glimpsed yet another expanse of young flesh much too pink from the sun.

Down Santa Monica to Kate's left a cheer went up, decidedly female in its shrillness, accompanied by much wolf-whistling. A darkly tanned, boyish female deputy sheriff Kate did not know rode by on a big bay horse; she was grinning foolishly. Her partner, balding and middle-aged, was shooing spectators back from the street with brief toots on his whistle; he too was grinning. Kate looked further up Santa Monica toward La Cienega and saw other brown clad deputies on motorcycles cruising slowly along the street. There was little for them to do; this playful, good-natured crowd, despite beer cans everywhere, showed no signs of rowdiness.

In the distance, toward La Cienega, there came a revving, a rumble of engines.

'It's starting, it's starting,' said the young man beside her.

Moments later, in front of Kate's bleachers, to rising cheers, leather-clad men on motorcycles, bearing American flags flying high on flagpoles decorated with colored streamers, came thundering past. The cycles turned around, performed intricate crisscross maneuvers among themselves, then thundered on down the Boulevard.

Behind them marched young people with a long black-lettered yellow banner:

CHRISTOPHER STREET WEST/LOS ANGELES GAY
PRIDE PARADE

And behind them another banner:

ALIVE WITH PRIDE IN '85

Then a white float glided into view, looking like whipped cream piled high, joyful music blaring from somewhere within, bold lettering on its side proclaiming America's newest city: CITY OF WEST HOLLYWOOD.

Kate could hear new cheers rising as the white float passed in stately slowness before her. Then the bleacher section erupted in shrill whistles and applause, and all around her the young men and women rose. Amid deafening sound that vibrated in her ears and under her feet she saw a banner:

PARENTS AND FRIENDS OF LESBIANS AND GAYS.

She stood, applauding with all the others, as the large contingent walked by holding their placards. Her eyes fastened on a man and woman, the man dark, the woman blonde, each with an arm around the young blonde girl between them; and she saw the sign the entwined hands of the parents were holding aloft:

WE LOVE OUR GAY DAUGHTER

Kate remained standing at the far end of the bleachers, watching as the group marched on down Santa Monica, hearing the cheers rise as they went.

She remained standing and watching, looking down Santa

Monica. As far as her tear-blinded eyes could see there were thousands of gay people. Thousands and thousands.

PANDORA PRESS

Pandora Press is a feminist press, an imprint of
Routledge & Kegan Paul. Our list is varied –
we publish new fiction, reprint fiction, history,
biography and autobiography, social issues,
humour – written by women and celebrating the
lives and achievements of women the world
over. For further information about Pandora
Press books, please write to the Mailing List
Dept. at Pandora Press, 11 New Fetter Lane,
London EC4P 4EE or in the USA at 35 West
35th Street, New York, NY 10001–291. Some
Pandora titles you will enjoy are:

AMATEUR CITY

by Katherine V. Forrest

A modern whodunnit, in the best traditions of
the genre.
'"Please look at me Miss O'Neil," Kate Delafield
sat with arms crossed, elbows resting on the
table. Her light blue eyes were not cold they
were not hostile, but they bored into Ellen's as
if she were seeing all the way to the back of
her head. There was a reason why a murderer
got across that hallway to safety, why you never
saw who it was."'
Kate Delafield, tough leader of the homicide
investigation team, soon discovers strong
motives for the killing of Fergus Parker in an
office united in its hatred of him. Her own
personal life is in crisis, and she finds her path
increasingly intersecting with that of chief
witness, Ellen O'Neil . . .

Pandora Women Crime Writers
April: LC8: 232pp
Paperback: 0-86358-200-1: £3.95

MURDER IN PASTICHE

by Marion Mainwaring

'A witty celebration of all that was best in the golden age of detective fiction.'
With nods in the direction of Agatha Christie, Dorothy L. Sayers, Ngaio Marsh and others, Marion Mainwaring produces a classic crime story in the styles of the most popular writers of detective fiction. Thinly disguised and thrown together on a transatlantic cruise, their most famous detectives attempt to solve the shipboard death of vindictive gossip columnist, Paul Price. You will meet Mr Atlas Poireau, Jerry Pason, Lord Simon Quinsey, Trajan Beare, Spike Bludgeon *et al*. Who did it? And perhaps more important who will solve the murder?

Pandora Women Crime Writers
May: LC8: 232pp
Paperback: 0-86358-206-0: £3.95

DEATH OF A DOLL

by Hilda Lawrence

High tension pervades this whodunnit set in a girls' hostel in America. A murder takes place in this claustrophobic all-female environment, and the classic female detection process is set in motion to solve it. Hilda Lawrence is well known to aficionados of crime fiction, as the author of *The Pavillion* and other excellent novels. *Death of a Doll* is unusual in having no single central narrator. It is also one of her finest novels.

Pandora Women Crime Writers
May: LCB: 232pp
Paperback: 0-86358-205-2: £3.95

GREEN FOR DANGER

by Christianna Brand

This is Christianna Brand's most celebrated
novel of crime and detection. In the brilliant
light of an operating theatre, during London's
war-time blitz, the patient is murdered – a
harmless old postman. And one of the six
members of the theatre staff must be the
murderer. Soon the whole hospital seethes with
mystery. A nurse, creeping back to the theatre
at dead of night in search of a clue encounters
a masked figure with surgical scalpel raised.
The tap of an unlit gas fire is turned on. Tablets
of morphine disappear. *Green for Danger* was
the basis for the film of the same name.

Pandora Women Crime Writers
May: 160pp
0-86358-208-7: £3.95